broken by lies

REBECCA SHEA

Just like our eyes, our
heart has a way of
adjusting to the dark.
Xo-
Rebecca
Shea

Broken by Lies

Copyright ©2015 Rebecca Shea Author, LLC

Createspace
ISBN-13: 978-0692354919
ISBN-10: 0692354913

Cover design by: Regina Wamba, Mae I Design
Edited by: Beth Lynne, Hercules Editing and Megan Hand
Formatted by: Angela McLaurin, Fictional Formats

broken by lies

dedication

To those who love the unlovable.

prologue

I INHALE THE fresh spring air as I start my walk home from work at the grocery store. The smell of moisture hangs in the air and small patches of snow are all that remain from the late spring snowstorm we received last week. Gravel crunches beneath my feet as I step along the shoulder of the only road that reaches from one end of this small town to the other. I live in a tiny trailer with my mom on the far edge of town. The small house sits next to White Lake, the town's namesake. For every day of my twenty-one years, we've lived in this piece of shit trailer. It's dilapidated and falling apart, but it's all we can afford, so I don't complain. I just make the best of our situation.

Once more, I kick at the gravel alongside the paved country road that leads to the lake and our little slice of broken-down home. It's dark out here in the dead of night, but the moon shines so brightly that you can easily see the road. I follow the shoulder, staying on the gravel so that I'm out of the way of any cars. It's not unusual not to see a single car pass me on the walk home. It is, however, unusual to see the flashing lights of a police car.

My heart begins to pump wildly when I see the lights turning down the gravel drive that leads to our trailer, and my feet take off in a full sprint. Stumbling a few times on the rocks, I near the trailer and hear my name being called.

"Emilia!" It's Carter, our landlord. "Emilia!" he hollers again. It's hard to believe anyone actually owns and rents the piece of shit trailer we live in, but he's always been good to us—and lenient when we don't have the rent on time.

"What's wrong?" I ask as I approach, out of breath. My eyes scan the trailer and find the front door open and flapping in the wind.

"It's your mom," Carter tells me, shaking his head. "When I came to collect the rent, she didn't answer. It's not like her, Em." He glances behind him at his dilapidated shack of an investment property. "The window was open, so I looked inside and, uh, saw her lying on the floor." Carter is visibly distraught as he runs a shaky hand through his silver hair and closes his eyes briefly.

Carter has always been like a grandfather to me. He's mild mannered but tough. Tall and strong, and nothing rattles him. Until now.

A police officer strings yellow crime scene tape around a tree, and I run straight past him as he begins yelling at me to stop. I run through the front door, and there lies my beautiful mother. On the living room floor. In a pool of blood. A black handgun sits next to her.

"No, no, no!" I scream. "Mama, no…" I gasp for air as I kneel down next to her. The blood is drying in her matted hair. It sinks into my knees, and I notice the blood has started to thicken and turn into a gel-like consistency on the floor. I pull her into my lap and hold her. I hold her and scream. I scream for her. I scream for me. I scream for how unfair life has been to us.

Sheriff Wilson runs through the front door and begs me to leave her. When I don't leave, he orders me to leave. I still don't. I can't leave her; she is all I have. I press my forehead to hers and cry. My tears fall in streams, landing on her face as I try to rationalize what's happening.

"Please, you can't leave me. Please," I whisper against her head.

"Emilia," Carter says quietly as he steps into the trailer. "Come on, girl; you don't need to be in here."

"I have to, Carter. She needs me. I need *her*," I wail. This can't be happening to us.

"Emilia, please. Come outside and talk to Sheriff Wilson. He has some questions."

Carter tugs on my arm, and I slide on the dingy, blood-smeared linoleum floor as I try to get up. Carter wraps an arm around my shoulder and guides me out of the trailer. My khaki pants are covered in blood, and my hands are shaking so bad I have to shove them in the pockets of my sweatshirt.

"Sheriff, this is Emilia, Carrie Adams' daughter."

"Ms. Adams." The sheriff nods at me with sympathy in his eyes.

My body begins to shake so badly; I can actually feel my knees knocking together. Carter holds me against him to steady me.

The sheriff sighs sympathetically. "I'm so sorry for your loss." He cringes when he says those words. "We're still piecing together all of the details, but it looks like suicide. The medical examiner will have to determine that, but no foul play is suspected," he says quietly.

"We don't own a gun," I mumble. Where would she get a gun? She wouldn't shoot herself and leave me alone. She told me she was actually feeling better, that the depression that used to eat her alive was finally at bay.

"Like I said, we'll let our crime scene technicians finish up, but the scene has been compromised." He looks at me harshly. "Mr. Wilson, I mean, Carter said there was a gun in her hand when he arrived."

"We didn't have a gun," I tell him again. "We didn't have access to a gun. We couldn't afford a gun. We could hardly eat. That gun in there is not ours."

Sheriff Wilson sighs and writes in his notebook.

"Do you have any other questions for her?" Carter asks. "I think she's in shock."

"That'll be all for now."

"Emilia, sit down," Carter says as he guides me to the large oak tree in front of our trailer. My limp body makes a loud thud when I sink to the ground. My chest feels like it's collapsing, and the air from my lungs has vanished. My limbs are stiff and I wonder if this is what it feels like to be in shock.

Time stands still as I watch police officers come and go, and I mumble answers to their questions as best as I can. Just as the morning sun begins to rise, I finally watch them wheel my mom from our trailer on a stretcher. Her body is encased in a large white plastic bag with a zipper up the front. I cry again when they put her into the back of an old county van marked "Medical Examiner," and then they drive away. She's gone. I'll never see her again, hug her again, or tell her I love her again.

I wipe at the tears as I curse the disease I believe took my mom. She has suffered from debilitating depression since the day my dad left, which was the day he found out she was pregnant with me. It was three days before she graduated from high school and gave up her dreams of going to college to raise me. She'd wanted to be a nurse. She might've been a good one. I've always felt a sense of guilt that I was the reason her life fell apart and that her dreams were shattered in order to raise me. However, the reality is that I pretty much raised her. For as long as I can remember, I was the one responsible for cooking, doing the laundry, and cleaning. I never knew the woman she claimed she used to be—fun and happy-go-lucky.

While she was never the perfect mother, she did her best raising me and insisted I do well in school. I've always been a straight A student, something I've prided myself on.

I glance down the drive and can almost see her standing there. In elementary school, she'd walk the quarter of a mile to the edge of the property every morning and wait with me for the bus to pick me up. And the afternoons that she wasn't asleep, lost in her depression, I'd find her waiting when the bus dropped me off. Those afternoons were few and far between, but I used to love seeing her waiting for me. Those were my happiest memories of her. Those days meant one thing—her depression was at bay, if only for a few hours.

Carter's voice pulls me from my memories. "I don't want you to go inside that trailer again, Emilia," he says quietly as he walks toward me. He has sat next to me for the last few hours, only leaving for a few minutes when they were unrolling the caution tape that now surrounds the trailer. "They've given me permission to get a few items from the bedroom for you while they finish up inside. You can stay in the spare bedroom at our place. I called Eve to let her know."

"What're they doing in there?" I manage to ask, my voice hoarse. My body is stiff and my head rests against the rough bark of the oak tree, the cool morning air pricking at my skin.

His hands are shoved in his front pockets as he looks down at me. "Just tell me what I can get for you," he sighs.

I quietly rattle off a small list of things, knowing they'll all fit into one shoulder bag. Carter disappears and is beside me a few minutes later. Or maybe it was an hour. Time bleeds together right now.

He tosses my bag in the back of his pick-up truck. "Let's go, Emilia," he says softly.

I glance up and stare at the rusty tin trailer, lost in a state of shock and denial. This broken down thing, as much as I've despised it, is the only home I've ever known. And mixed with my grief is a sharp panic—what will happen to me and where I will go? What is my life now?

"I'm going to sit here for a while," I mutter. "I need to be alone. I'll be over in a bit."

"Come straight to the house," he says firmly. "If you're not there in an hour, I'm coming back. And, Emilia, don't go back inside that trailer."

I just nod.

He hesitates before climbing into his pick-up truck and leaving, a trail of dust following his old truck down the gravel road. Within a few minutes, everyone is finally gone, leaving me sitting against this oak tree. Realization finally sets in...

I am truly *alone*.

chapter one

Emilia

I FEEL LIKE I've entered an oven as I step off the Greyhound bus. The Phoenix heat scorches my lungs and stings my eyes. It's nine o'clock in the evening; I can't imagine what it's like during the day when the sun is out. I stop on the sidewalk, trying to get my bearings, and I'm bumped from behind by a large man that grunts at me and forcefully nudges me out of his way. Palm trees line the city street in front of me, and there is a small line of taxis parked in front of the dimly lit station. With the little money I have, I know I'll be taking a city bus and not a taxi.

I run my finger over the scribbled address on the crumpled paper before tucking it safely back into my pocket. With no plan and no idea where I'm staying tonight, I stand in line at the one open window at the ticket counter. A light sheen of sweat blankets my face, and I'm thinking that wearing jeans on a thirty-nine-hour bus ride to Phoenix in the middle of June probably wasn't the best idea. I'm sticky and uncomfortable and just want a shower and sleep.

The man in front of me steps away from the window, and I approach nervously. The woman behind the counter is old and short, wearing thick eyeglasses and a pair of pants that are about two sizes smaller than she needs. She doesn't make eye contact with me, but barks questions and commands in her raspy smoker's voice. "Next. Step up. Where're you goin'?"

She punches the keys on the dirty keyboard in front of her. I clear my throat and step closer so she can hear me. "I don't know." My voice is weak, timid.

"Well, how can I help you if you don't know where you're going?" Her tone is condescending. She looks up from her keyboard and meets my eyes indifferently.

"I just got off that bus." I point toward the oversized silver bus that is sitting at the curb. "I'm staying here in Phoenix, but I just need a recommendation for a safe place to stay that's in my price range."

Her shoulders fall, and an audible sighs escapes her mouth as she studies me. "Anything affordable isn't going to be safe," she grumbles. "Where are you from?"

"White Lake, Illinois."

"Figures," she mumbles under her breath as she looks me up and down from head to toe before typing away on her keyboard again. "Look, I don't know what your budget is, but here's a list of motels that start at thirty a night and go up to a hundred. Stay off of Van Buren, girl; they'd eat you alive over there." She chuckles to herself and shoves three pieces of paper at me under the slat in the glass window.

"Thank you." I smile at her politely and take the papers. Standing underneath the street light, I sort through them, then move toward the bus stop with the one bag I brought. It holds three changes of clothes, a notebook, three books, and my wallet. That's all I own. The few items I left behind were of little to no value to me and would've been more weight to worry about.

I sit nervously on the scorching metal bench and wait, adrenaline coursing through me. Using the large map on the side of the bus shelter, I mentally jot down the three buses it'll take to get me to the strip of motels that hopefully will have a cheap room available for a few days. When the bus pulls up to the curb, I get on and deposit my money before taking a seat in the middle of the mostly empty space.

Public transportation is alike in most cities, as well as the people who ride it—you can see the exhaustion written across their faces. I lean my head against the window and focus on the passing cars and businesses as we snake through the dark streets of Phoenix. An hour and two transfers later, I arrive at my final stop. Pulling the straps of my bag onto my shoulder, I step off and out onto the dark street.

I can see the signs for the motels just ahead, about two and a half blocks away. Walking briskly toward the bright signs, I keep my eyes glued to my destination. A bed and a shower are so close that I can almost feel my sore muscles begin to relax. The motels are just off a major interstate and sit along a service road. There's a lot of traffic, which makes me more comfortable in this foreign city. As the lights get closer, I finally step off the sidewalk and across the black asphalt parking lot toward the small building. A neon light flashes the word "office," and I increase my speed, jetting through the parked cars. Even in the evening you can feel the summer heat penetrating the surface of the blacktop, right through my sandals. I wriggle my toes against the thin soles of my shoes.

When I push the glass door open, I'm greeted with a blast of cool air. For the first time in an hour, I feel like I can breathe and my lungs respond with a deep inhale. I take a couple of deep breaths, then tilt my face up toward the air conditioning vent in the ceiling, hoping it dries the sweat on my face.

"Can I help you?" an older man with gray hair asks as he steps out from behind a closed door.

I startle. "Hi. Um. Yes. I need a room for a couple of nights."

"Two?" He takes me in, glancing over the rim of his glasses before looking back to his computer.

"Yes, just two nights for now, please."

"You from around here?" he inquires.

"No." I swallow. "Illinois."

"I'll need your license and credit card."

"I have a picture ID and cash." *Please let that be enough.* I can't imagine trying to find another place now. I reach into my bag to pull out my wallet.

He pauses and looks over the counter at me. "We don't do cash business here. I've been working real hard to clean this place up." He pauses and looks me over again.

"I don't have a credit card," I stutter, as panic sets in.

He exhales loudly and stares at me, his eyes becoming sympathetic. "For cash, it'll be one hundred and fifty dollars."

I swallow hard. All I have is two hundred dollars and that won't get me back to Illinois if things don't go well here. "Uh…" I turn and look out the large glass windows to the motel next door, the vacancy sign flashing bright in the dark. I wonder if it's any cheaper. It's rundown and dingy—more so than this Motel 6, and it's getting late. I fidget nervously, trying to make up my mind.

"Okay." I turn back and smile at him. I pull the cash from my wallet, count out the one hundred fifty, and slide it across the counter.

He prints me out a receipt that I shove in my bag and slides a key card across the counter. "I don't want any trouble here. You look like a good girl. Go to your room and stay there," he says, and retreats back behind the closed door he had come from just a few minutes earlier.

A sticky note stuck to the front of the keycard states that I'm in room one hundred forty-three. I pull the straps from my bag a little higher on my shoulder and step back out into the hot, heavy air. Following the sidewalk that winds around the parking lot, I walk briskly as the numbers on the doors ascend.

There's a group of four men outside one of the rooms, smoking and laughing, and my heart rate increases. *Leave me alone, just leave me alone.* But as I approach, they all fall silent. Stepping around them, I keep my eyes focused on the sidewalk. My heart pounds wildly in my chest, and my pace quickens as I glance again at the numbers.

127... 129...

135... 137... 139...

My panic begins to ease slightly. *Only three doors away.* Chancing a quick glance over my shoulder, I hear the squeaky hinges of a door opening just as I run square into the person exiting. I startle and try to step back as I begin apologizing profusely, but firm hands grip my shoulders, not allowing me to move.

"I'm so sorry," I gasp. The keycard falls from my hand and lands at the feet of the man I nearly ran over. Looking down, my eyes take in his expensive black shoes, the keycard resting on the ground just in front of him.

His hands release my shoulders, and I lunge for the keycard, but he's too quick, reaching down and picking it up before I can get to it. His tan fingers wrap around the cheap plastic as he stands up. In shock for a moment, I finally pull myself up and meet his amber eyes.

"Are you okay?" He narrows his honey-colored eyes on me, and I take in his gray dress pants, black shirt, no tie. His hair is short, but slightly wispy on top—a little messy, not perfectly in place. His skin is golden brown, as if he's been on a tropical vacation. His tan skin makes those amber eyes pop against his dark eyelashes. His square jaw is sprinkled with just enough hair to show he hasn't shaved today, but it's his dimples that take my breath away. He's so well put together I'd guess he was in his thirties. He may be the most beautiful man I've ever laid eyes on, but he screams money, power—danger.

"Are you okay?" he asks again, tilting his head at me as I drink him in.

"Oh, um… yes, sorry… just nervous." I look away from him and down to my fidgeting hands.

He glances behind me at the men on the sidewalk and then back to me as if piecing things together. "Are they harassing you?" He gestures with his head.

"No." I shake my head. "I'm just tired. It's been a really long day. I'm sorry I bumped into you," I say timidly. I extend my hand, palm up in an unspoken gesture for him to return my keycard. My hand shakes as he looks between the card in his hand and me. His thumb flicks at the little yellow sticky note before he turns around and walks toward the door marked one hundred forty-three. He inserts the keycard and pushes the door open, holding it for me.

My heart stammers in my chest as I approach cautiously. I notice the expensive watch on his wrist, which peeks out from his dress shirt, and the light, luxurious smell of what can only be designer cologne. The scent paralyzes me—so intoxicating that I want to press my face to his neck and breathe him in.

Everything inside me—my good sense, my gut—screams at me not to walk toward that door, but I go against my better judgment. In three quick strides, I'm standing at the open door to my motel room as his amber eyes follow me. Brushing against him, I slide by and reach for the lights on the wall just inside the door. Only a small bedside lamp illuminates the room. I notice the musty smell as I glance around at the old furniture.

"Close this door and lock it," he says, pulling the keycard from the door. He steps just over the threshold and into the room, reaching out to me with the keycard. "Don't open this door for anybody. Understand?"

I swallow hard and nod. His fingers are warm against my palm as he places the keycard in my hand. My fingers instinctively close and trap his hand in mine. Rooted in place, he scans the room as if searching for something or someone. With no other words of warning or even a goodbye, he pulls his hand free and steps back through the door, closing it behind him with a loud bang.

Did that just happen?

I scramble across the old stained blue carpet to the large window. Leaning across a small table, I pull down one of the slats of the cheap metal blinds to look for the beautiful stranger. I easily find him standing just outside my door, his mobile phone pressed to his ear. His full lips barely move as he speaks into the slim phone. Catching my breath, I let go of the blinds and move quickly back to the door, at first fumbling with, but eventually inserting the chain lock just as he instructed. Glancing through the peephole, I watch him step away, then I lean back against the door, closing my eyes and burning the memory of his face into my brain.

It takes me a few minutes to remember why I came here in the first place—bed and shower. But a shower will have to wait. Exhausted does not describe how I'm feeling. I strip down to my panties and bra and pull the covers back on the double bed as I slide in. The mattress is lumpy, but better than the one I slept on at home. I lay in the eerie silence for a few minutes, the stranger's words of warning on repeat in my head. My heart is beating wildly, and I don't understand why. I don't even know this guy, but he ignited a feeling deep inside me—a feeling I thought I'd never feel again. Men were trouble for us Adams women—they had a tendency to skip town to chase their dreams and leave behind broken hearts. I sigh deeply as images of the beautiful man flash through my head. And even though I'm drained, it still takes a few minutes to calm down before I finally fall into a deep sleep.

I SIT UP straight out of a dead sleep when I hear the banging on my door. I glance at the old alarm clock on the bedside table as it flashes three thirty-seven a.m. My heart is pounding with fear, and my mouth instantly dries. Who the hell could it be? I scurry from the bed to look through the peephole. It's still dark outside, and I can feel the hot Phoenix air pushing its way through the flimsy motel door. Three Hispanic men are standing just outside, and the older man in the front pounds on my door again, startling me. I hear the squeaky hinges from the room next door open and the three men laugh as they step away from my door and move toward the one that just opened. They're speaking Spanish. The sound of those squeaky hinges and the thud of a door closing tell me they've entered the room and found who they were looking for—not me.

Thank God.

I take a step back and lean against the rough-textured wall as I try to calm down. Drops of sweat roll down my temples, and I realize for the first time how hot it is in this room, even though the old air conditioner is rattling away. Pushing myself off the wall, I walk to the small unit and turn the knob to "high." I let the cool air blow directly on my face. It does little to break the heat in the room. Grabbing my bag from the table, I head to the bathroom to shower. My heart is still racing a million miles an hour; there's no way I'll be able to go back to sleep.

The bathroom is smaller than the one Mom and I had in our trailer. There's an extra small sink, a toilet, and a shower so tiny there's hardly room to turn around in it. I reach in and turn the water to cold, but even the cold water here is scalding hot. The showerhead is so low the water sprays my chest instead of my head. Lowering myself to wet my hair, I use the small bottle of shampoo that the motel supplied and lather it into my hair. There's no conditioner, so I'll have to fight with the tangles in my long hair. I'm used to this. Even at home, conditioner was a rarely seen luxury. The once white washcloth left for me is stained a dingy shade of grey, but it's the least of my concerns. I quickly wash and rinse my body of the sudsy soap. Drying off, I send a quiet prayer to my mom. She wouldn't approve of me doing this, but I have no other options—I have no one.

The girl in the mirror looks back at me. She looks so lost, and I chuckle at the thought of my lost hopes and dreams. What are those? I can't even remember. I had wanted to study law, maybe become a lawyer. That was before I realized we were dirt poor, and I had to take care of my depressed mother. We had no car, barely had food, and most of that was given to me by Mr. O'Sullivan, my manager at the grocery store.

Everyone compliments me and tells me I'm beautiful, but I just don't see it. I'm tall and lanky with mousy, light brown hair. My eyes are hazel; sometimes brown and sometimes green—but always dull, tired, and lifeless. I'm sure if I cared about my appearance, I could make myself look decent. But at home my only concern was working enough hours to keep the shitty trailer and taking a class or two at the community college so that I could eventually consider going to law school.

When Carter was cleaning out the trailer after my mom died, he found a small notebook with my dad's name and information in it. When he handed it to me, he did so with hesitation. Everyone in White Lake knew my father, but no one talked about him. I'd heard he was an only child and that his parents had moved away when I was just a baby. The one time I asked about him, when I was around sixteen, my mom told me he bailed on her after she told him she was pregnant with me. And by bailed, I mean he moved away for college to chase his dreams, and my mom stayed behind in White Lake to raise me. She said he was three years older than she was, and in college, and that's where the conversation ended. Now I have his name, and with the help of the computer and librarian at the public library, I have an address—here in Phoenix.

I sit at the small table in the room, dressed and waiting for the sun to come up. Pulling out the paper map that I got on the city bus last night, I map out the route to my dad's house. He lives in North Central Phoenix. It'll take two buses with one transfer, an easy trip from here, so I relax a little as the sun begins to peek through the blinds at around a quarter to six. I stuff the book I was trying to read back into my bag and pull out my wallet. Not wanting to leave my bag in the open, I shove it in the top drawer of the rickety, faux wood dresser and take a deep breath.

Time to go meet my father.

Thirty-five minutes and two buses later, I'm standing at the corner of an intersection in a gorgeous neighborhood full of massive ranch homes. Downtown Phoenix rests in the backdrop behind these perfectly manicured lawns. I walk the winding neighborhood streets to the address scribbled on the piece of paper that I'm clutching in my hand.

The area is quiet as I stroll nervously toward the house at the end of the street. I recheck the address. This is it. The house is gorgeous; stucco with stone columns that create an enormous front porch. A black Mercedes Benz SUV sits in the driveway and giant clay pots full of colorful flowers line the paved sidewalk that leads to the front door. Hesitantly, I walk up the flagstone sidewalk and stand just outside the enormous wood door. My heart races as my fingers hover over the doorbell before I finally press it and take a step back. I take a few deep breaths, willing myself to calm down when I hear the shuffling of footsteps. My mind races with fear and unanswered questions. *Will he know I'm his daughter? What will he look like? Do I look like him?* With the click of the deadbolt, the front door swings open.

I gasp. There's no mistaking that the man who greets me is my father. His hazel eyes meet mine, and I can't help but notice how tall he is, like me. He has to be at least six foot four and fit. He is lean but muscular. I can see his build easily through his fitted dress shirt and tie. He has dark brown hair with a sprinkling of gray along each temple. In his suit, he looks every part the distinguished businessman I assumed he'd be—everything my mom was not.

"Can I help you?" His voice is hoarse, and he clears his throat as I stand and take in my father. His eyes narrow slightly as if he *might* see a hint of recognition.

"Hi," I mumble as I wipe my hands on the bottom of my dress. Realizing how ridiculous I must look, I pretend I'm smoothing out the skirt rather than wiping my sweaty hands. "Um, I'm Emilia."

"Emilia?" He tilts his head and studies me.

"Yeah, Emilia," I repeat. He genuinely has no idea who I am. "Oh God, you didn't even know my name?" I drop my eyes. He opens the door wider and steps out onto the front porch as if to get a better look at me. Finally, his eyes widen in recognition, and then he glances around as if looking for someone else.

"She died two months ago," I whisper. He inhales sharply. "I'm sorry to stop by like this, but I didn't have your number, and honestly, I didn't know if you'd want to see me… but…" I fidget with the hem of my dress as I stumble over my words.

He stands firm and watches me. His jaw muscles tighten as his eyes take me in from head to toe—judging me. He doesn't speak. He just looks at me. "How did she die?" he asks me quietly as he glances over my shoulder, scanning the street behind me.

"Suicide." I answer him like it's something he should know. But he wouldn't know. He didn't know anything about her life, about our life after he left. He nods his head. "I don't have anyone now that she's gone, and I just wanted…"

"You need to leave." His tone is firm and commanding, but not loud. "Now."

Leave? I'm completely caught off guard, and I struggle to speak. Tears burn at the back of my eyes, and I instantly feel my chin begin to tremble. "I came all the way from Illinois. Can we just talk for a few minutes? Please."

He shakes his head once. "Now is not a good time."

"When will be a good time?" I ask quickly, in a panic, as he backs toward his front door.

"I don't know. Please don't stop by unannounced again," he says before promptly closing the large front door with a loud bang.

Tears fall as my throat tightens and a quiet sob escapes. I wipe my cheeks as I step back off the front porch and stumble my way down the driveway. I don't want him to see me crying. I never needed my father growing up. As much as I wanted him, and as much as I'd like to say I don't need him now, I do. Disappointment and hurt fill the space in my heart that I opened up to love my father.

My heart beats rapidly as I retrace my steps back those couple of blocks to the bus stop. The day they wheeled Mom out of our trailer was the loneliest I've ever felt—until today. Until right now. Knowing that you have a parent that is alive but rejects you—wants nothing to do with you—has to be the loneliest feeling in the world. But to have your own flesh and blood deny you is definitely the most hurtful. Even when my mom was lost in her world of depression, she still loved and wanted me. We had nothing, but she gave me love. It was all she gave, and yet I miss it. God, I miss it... I miss her.

chapter two

Alex

PULLING INTO THIS shitty motel off the interstate, I throw the gearshift into park and take the package out of the center console. I stare at the door marked one forty-one and grind my teeth in frustration. This is the last swap. I'm not normally down in the weeds like this, but with half our guys incarcerated or dead in the last week, it's been left to me to handle some of the dirty work. *Fuck.* I hate this part of the job—this is not what I do. I have a master's degree, for fuck's sake.

I want this done fast and error free, which is why I'm here. I make sure my gun is loaded, and I slide it into the waistband of my pants. Then I scan the parking lot for anything suspicious before I exit the car and knock on the door. The flimsy wood door swings open, and Hector greets me.

"Alejandro." Hector and his guys deal the drugs my family and associates bring across the border. He and my father have been in "business" together for over twenty-five years. And even though my father trusts him, I don't.

He nods and steps aside to let me enter, eyeing the wrapped package in my hand. Strutting to the dresser, he pulls a fast food paper bag out of the top drawer. "*Es todo lo que hay.*"

"It's all in here? All fifty?" I open the paper bag and glance at the neatly bound stacks of cash inside.

"*Sí.*"

I hand him the wrapped package of pure black tar heroin, and he grins. This is twice in two days that I've had to swap drugs for cash. Hector's men stand quietly behind him while keeping a careful eye on me. All it would take is one word, one wrong move, and they wouldn't hesitate to take me out. The difference between me and Hector and his men is that I stand out like a sore thumb on this side of town in my Range Rover and my designer clothes. I grimace when I see a young girl who looks no older than sixteen or seventeen stumble out of the restroom and sidle up next to Hector.

God, have some fucking respect for yourself.

I've seen enough. Not wanting to draw any unneeded attention to myself, or Hector, I decide it's best to leave quickly. "I have to go. *Gracias*, Hector." I shove the bag of cash into the waistband of my pants, next to my gun.

"*Mijo*, I'm sorry to hear about your father's *situation.*" That's a polite way of acknowledging his incarceration. "Thank you for keeping up your family's end of the bargain."

I don't know if his apology is genuine, or if he's making a point that our business is weak at the moment. Men like Hector will try to capitalize on my family's weakness, so I hide my distrust, nodding politely and closing the door behind me.

As I unlock my SUV, something catches my eye across the parking lot. It's *her*. The scared girl I saw last night. The one I can't stop thinking about. She's walking toward the frontage road that runs alongside the freeway. Damn, she looks good, and she sure as hell shouldn't be out here. Wearing a short green dress, her long legs extending for miles.

I get in the car and back out, again making sure I'm not being followed—worst part of this job is never knowing who might be lurking in the shadows, ready to take me out. I slow down as I pull up alongside her. I can already tell that something is wrong from the way she carries herself. Her head is dropped forward, and her long hair falls gently into her face, but it's when she wipes the tears from under her eyes that I know she's not okay.

Fuck, this isn't my problem, I think as I pass her slowly. As I pull further away from her, though, something inside me stirs. I step on the brake and watch her through the rearview mirror. Her shoulders are slouched in defeat.

"Fuuuuuccckkkk," I hiss as I grip the steering wheel and turn the car around. Rolling down my window as I approach her, I try to sound concerned and not like I'm trying to pick her up. "Hey, is everything okay?"

She keeps her head down and continues walking, not acknowledging me. *Good girl, keep your defenses up.* As she wipes her cheeks, her pace quickens, and I find myself once again doubling back to catch up to her, this time passing her.

Swerving the SUV to the shoulder of the road, I jump out and double back toward her just as she approaches me. Her eyes meet mine briefly, but instantly fall back to her feet. The fear I saw last night has been replaced with sadness.

"Are you going to answer me?" I plant myself directly in her path so that she'll either stop or run into me.

She stops a short distance back, but still doesn't look at me. "What do you want?"

"I want to know if you're okay."

She remains silent.

"Where are you going? Let me give you ride." I want her to say yes, although, if she says no, I'd almost be more proud than if she accepts.

She remains planted on the baking asphalt. It has to be at least a hundred and ten degrees already, and the pale skin on her shoulders is tinged a light shade of pink.

"I don't know," she whispers, her chin beginning to quiver.

I frown at her. "You don't know where you're going?" She shakes her head and wipes her nose with the back of her hand. It doesn't take me long to react. "Get in the car."

"I can't. I don't know you," she says as more tears fall from her eyes. Instinctively, I reach out and swipe her cheek with my thumb. Surprisingly, she doesn't pull away like I expect her to— like she should.

"I'm not going to hurt you. Just get in the car until you figure out where you're going, and I'll drive you there." I wrap my fingers around her wrist, gently tugging her toward me. Finally, she lifts her head and her eyes meet mine. She's still every bit the stunning woman I remember from last night, but today, she is a beautiful broken girl that I need to help.

She nods once and follows me to my SUV. I don't release her wrist; instead, I loosen my grip and let my hand fall into hers. Our palms connect, and she tries to pull away, but I hold tight.

Approaching the car, I release her hand and gently pull the strap of her bag off of her shoulder. I open the front passenger door, holding it open for her, and she pauses.

"Why are you helping me? I mean, I met you for two seconds last night."

It's a damn good question. One I wish I knew the answer to. "I don't know. All I know is I can't leave you out here with nowhere to go."

She swallows hard and forces a small smile before stepping up into the leather seat.

Opening the back door, I set her bag on the back seat, wondering what's inside, as it's so light. "Is this all you have?"

"That's it," she says bleakly as she closes the door and settles into the front seat. She adjusts the vents, allowing the air to blow directly on her face, her long hair billowing behind her. Finally, she allows her head to fall back against the headrest, and she momentarily closes her eyes. Her chin still quivers, and I watch the muscles in her neck constrict as she swallows and exhales deeply.

As I slide into my seat, she's buckling herself in, and I can't help but notice how thin she is. When did she last eat? I shouldn't care, but I do. She crosses her legs at her ankles, her pale skin standing out against the black leather seats. I put the car in drive and head toward my downtown condo until she tells me to drive her somewhere else.

"I'm Alex," I say, keeping my focus on the road and the cars around me. Out of the corner of my eye, I see her turn her head to look at me.

"Emilia." Her voice is just over a whisper.

Emilia; beautiful Emilia.

She turns her head away from me to stare out the passenger window. I let the silence fill the air between us, choosing to forgo music. I have a million questions, but I don't want to overwhelm her.

"It's beautiful here," she says. "So different from where I'm from."

I bite at this opportunity to get some questions in, to find out more about her. "Where are you from?"

She folds her hands in her lap, picking at the skin on the side of her thumb until it's almost raw. "White Lake, Illinois." She looks at me with eyes full of despair.

"Never heard of it." But it sounds small, and she seems like a small-town girl.

"Most people haven't. If you blink while driving through, you'd miss it." A small laugh escapes her.

"What brought you to Phoenix?"

She swallows and glances out the passenger window again. "I came to find my dad."

"Did you find him?" I ask curiously.

"Yep. Didn't go exactly how I envisioned it," she says, and her voice cracks. Her shoulders begin to shake, and I can tell she's fighting with herself while trying not to cry—again maintaining control of her emotions.

"Hey, he'll come around. When's the last time you saw him?"

"Never." Her mouth turns into a hard line. "I've never met him—until this morning."

"Really?" I can't imagine that, never knowing my father.

She nods, that heartbreak in her eyes again. "Yeah. I've known of him… heard stories about him, but I never met him until today…" She pauses.

"So, now what? You're going to go back to your family in Illinois?" I navigate the busy Phoenix streets as we get closer to downtown, being mindful of the cars behind me in the rearview mirror.

"I don't have any family. My mom died a couple of months ago." She pauses again, her lip quivering. "I don't know what I'm going to do." She presses her lips together when her voice breaks with emotion.

I chance a quick glance at her, but she stares straight ahead, lost in her thoughts. We both remain quiet as we near my condo, and I push the button on the steering wheel, triggering the large metal gate to roll open at the entrance to the parking garage.

"I should get out here," she says quietly, reaching for the door handle. "I'll catch a bus to the Greyhound."

I step on the brake, the car stopping quickly. "You just said you had no one to go home to. Where is the Greyhound going to take you?"

She hesitates before shrugging. "I'm not sure. I have fifty dollars, so wherever that'll take me, I guess."

Taking a deep breath, I pull forward into the garage and park in my assigned space. "Fifty dollars isn't going to get you anywhere you want to go. You're welcome to stay with me until you figure out what you're doing, or where you're going. It's just me in this enormous condo. I have the space and… I've been thinking of getting a roommate, so this works out perfectly." I have no idea why I offered this invitation to a beautiful stranger, to someone I've just met, but something tells me she needs me, and maybe I need her too.

She blinks at me in confusion. "I can't be your roommate." She reaches for the door handle. "You don't even know me. I barely have money for a bus ticket. How can I pay rent?"

I shrug. "I don't need the money."

She studies me cautiously, looking for any indication of who I really am. She'll never know I'm really a monster.

"I can't do that. I can't accept that offer." She seems caught off guard by my concern for her well-being, as she appears to consider my offer.

"And I can't let you wander the streets alone—headed to a bus station to take a bus to nowhere." My fingers grip the leather-bound steering wheel in frustration.

"I'll figure it out," she says, unbuckling her seatbelt.

"You'll figure it out while you stay here. End of discussion." My voice is firm... commanding. She's too proud to admit that she needs me, and I sure as hell am not letting her walk away.

Her eyes open wide at my orders, and I unlock the car doors, stepping out into the parking garage. I study each car, making sure I recognize them, then I instantly relax when I see Saul peek around the corner and nod at me before his eyes lock on Emilia.

I open the car door for her and she steps down hesitantly. She wobbles on shaky legs, grabbing my arm to balance herself. I reach for her bag in the backseat when she finally steps toward me, catching me off guard.

"Thank you, Alex," she says. Her voice is quiet, but her eyes are full of sincerity.

"You're welcome, Emilia." I love the way her name sounds, rolling off my tongue.

I CARRY HER bag as we ride the elevator to my penthouse condo on the eleventh floor. Her shoulders are hunched forward and her thin arms wrapped tightly around her waist. I stand behind her, watching her every move. The elevator carries us up the old brick building that was recently converted to condominiums. I purchased the entire top floor and had it custom designed, not that I really give a shit about any of that.

When the elevator opens directly into my foyer, I step around her, holding the doors open as she steps inside. Her eyes immediately widen as she takes in her surroundings, and I feel a swell of satisfaction inside of me. She follows closely behind me as I step through the foyer and down the short hall that leads into the extravagant kitchen—so large, it's damn near obnoxious. A shame I never use it.

"This kitchen is bigger than our entire trailer," she says breathily as she runs her hand across the smooth granite countertop. "Your house is beautiful." Her lips tighten into a small smile. It's the first time I've seen her smile, and it's stunning; she's stunning.

"Thank you," I respond shyly. I've never been embarrassed of my wealth, but knowing that she has absolutely nothing and yet she compliments the wealth I've inherited entirely illegally, and at the demise of many people, I suddenly feel guilty.

"You can stay in the guest room over here." I point toward an open door as I walk across the kitchen and down the hall to the spare bedroom that sits just off the main living room. "Except it won't be a guest room anymore. It'll be your room."

I don't look at her to see her reaction to that statement; I just set her bag at the foot of the bed and glance around the room. The walls are stark white—not much life in here—but it's fully furnished and has never been used. I don't even know why I had this room furnished—it's not like I ever have visitors—but now,

I'm suddenly glad I did.

She brushes up against me as she slides through the doorway and into the room. "It's beautiful, so bright." She steps over to the large window that overlooks the outside patio.

Not as beautiful as you.

As she stands at the window, the summer sunlight shines down on her. Her dark hair hangs long against her back and her thin legs poke out from her short dress. She looks like a piece of heaven, an angel, against the long white sheer curtains that hang from both sides of the window. Everything about her is innocent, natural—stunning.

"Make yourself at home. I'll be down the hall in my office, getting some work done." I gesture down the long hallway. "Feel free to check out the condo."

"Alex." She says my name, and I freeze. "Thank you." Her voice wavers, and I nod at her as I leave and find my way to my office.

I spend the next hour checking emails and fielding calls from my father's very expensive defense attorneys. Trying to run a fucking criminal organization damn near by myself is beyond stressful. I've always just been the money guy. I handle the money, and I purchase real estate. I don't arrange for fucking shipments of heroin or bundles of weed. I don't make the deals or deliver the goods. I don't smuggle people across the border, and I sure as hell don't murder people. But today, I've been fucking arranging all of this.

Sitting back in my leather chair, I lace my fingers behind my head. I feel a headache coming on, and with as much work as I still have to do, I don't have time for a headache. As my thoughts wander, I find it hard to concentrate. I'm drawn to the beautiful girl down the hall.

Pushing myself away from the large glass-top desk, I head to the kitchen and grab two bottles of water. I half expect to see her in the living room, on the couch watching TV, or find her roaming the condo as she settles in. Instead, I hear sniffles coming from her bedroom. Her door isn't shut all the way, and I peer inside, finding her curled into a ball in the middle of the large bed. Her dark hair is splayed on the pillow; another pillow is pressed up against her stomach, her arms wrapped tightly around it.

I stand for a moment, unsure what to do. I almost feel like a bastard when I knock softly on the door to get her attention. Maybe I should've just stayed out of it, let her cry.

She doesn't move. "Door's open," she says quietly, wiping under her eyes.

"Are you all settled?" I glance around the room and see nothing personal of hers except a leather-bound notebook on the nightstand.

"Yeah, didn't take long... I don't have much." She pushes herself to an upright position on the bed. Her cheeks are flush and the whites of her eyes are pink from crying.

"What can I do to help you, Emilia? What do you need?" I wonder what it is she truly needs, aside from the basics of shelter and food.

"Nothing. You've done enough for me already."

"I haven't done anything."

"You're letting me stay here, which is very kind and, honestly, very unsettling." She lets out a little laugh. "I don't know you. I know nothing about you, except your name is Alex. And quite frankly, this entire situation scares me a little bit." It's the first time she's been open with me, and I want to put her fears to rest.

"What do you want to know?" I lean back against the cool brick wall and study her.

She sits cross-legged on the bed, her skirt tucked just inside her knees. "Do you always pick up girls from the side of a road and bring them home?"

"Nope. This was definitely a first." I chuckle.

"How old are you?"

"Twenty-seven."

"What's your last name?"

I hesitate, wondering what she'd find if she Googled me. "Estrada."

"What do you do—your job?"

Shit. My family runs a fucking cartel. We smuggle drugs, people, guns—you know, living the American dream. I barely contain my cringe as I half-lie, "I own real estate and am co-owner of a transportation business."

That wasn't so hard.

She eyes me cautiously. "So, you're rich." She glances out the open bedroom door into the condo that's overbearing and way too extravagant for someone my age.

"I have money, enough of it that I'm comfortable, but I'm hardly rich." I don't know why I said that, but it's true. While I have cars, a luxury condo, and more money than I can spend in my lifetime, there are so many things I'm missing. The things that truly make a person rich, I will never have—a nine-to-five job, a normal relationship, a family.

A spark of amusement hits her eyes. "What's your favorite color?"

I give a small smile. "Blue."

"Do you have any siblings?" she continues.

My brows furrow at this sudden onslaught of random questions. Before I can answer, she jumps in with the one I'm not sure I'll ever be able to answer honestly.

"What scares you?"

I hesitate, wondering how to answer. Never show your fears. This is how I was raised. Men don't show fear and they never talk about what scares them. "Nothing. I mean, I haven't really thought about that." I shrug. "Nothing scares me." *Everything scares me. My life scares me. The fact that I have to look over my shoulder every time I step out of my house scares the living shit out of me.*

Pushing forward off the exposed brick wall, I come to where she sits on the bed. As I get closer, her eyes drop from mine to her hands that are resting on the pillow in her lap. I stand over her thin body and drink in her beauty.

You scare me, Emilia. The feeling to protect and care for a beautiful stranger that I just met scares the living shit out of me.

"What scares *you*?" I ask her quietly.

She looks up at me, her bright hazel eyes glistening with tears. "Everything," she whispers. "Everything scares me."

I want to run my fingers across her cheek to wipe her tears, but I hold back. "Don't be scared. I won't let anything hurt you."

It's the first of many lies I will tell Emilia.

chapter three

Emilia

"ARE YOU HUNGRY?"

I startle at the sound of his voice and quickly close the leather-bound notebook I was making notes in, laying it on the bed next to me. "Not really," I answer as my stomach growls, blowing my lie.

He shakes his head and smiles. "You're a terrible liar," he says, leaning against the doorframe. He's changed into a pair of black basketball shorts and a tight gray t-shirt. Dressed down, he looks even more muscular, lean, and tall. He must stand at least six foot three. His skin is perfectly tan, the color of caramel, and his lips are full, soft looking.

Why am I looking at his lips?

"When's the last time you ate?" His eyes travel down to my bony legs, which stick out from underneath my short sundress.

I actually have to think about the last time I ate, and it was two days ago, before I got on that Greyhound bus. Funny thing is, I'm not even hungry. The stress of not knowing where your life is heading must stave off the hunger pains.

"A couple days ago." I'm almost embarrassed at the admission.

"*Days?*" His eyes widen in surprise. "Get up." His normally relaxed voice is rigid, firm. I follow his order and swing my legs over the side of the bed, my feet hitting the cool stone floor as I slide off. I look around for my sandals that I've kicked off, but don't find them.

"You don't need your shoes. Come on." I follow him into the gorgeous kitchen. "Here." He slides a paper menu at me across the kitchen island as I perch on one of the tall barstools. "Do you like Thai food?"

"I've never had Thai."

"What? Really?" He laughs.

"Do you remember where I told you I was from?" I raise an eyebrow. "There isn't even a McDonald's within twenty miles of my hometown."

He smirks at me. I hate nothing more than cocky arrogance in men. I didn't get that vibe from him before, but right now, he looks disgusted with me. I can only imagine what he thinks of this little hick Illinois girl, dressed in secondhand clothes, not a dime to her name, never having eaten Thai food.

"So, what do you like to eat?" he asks with a raised eyebrow.

Anger sets in, and I narrow my eyes at him. "Judging from the looks of this condo, I'm guessing you've never been poor, have you, Alex? When you're poor, you eat whatever you can find. In my case, I was responsible for our meals. Most of the time, it was peanut butter sandwiches or pasta. Not because I couldn't cook, but because that's what we could afford. So unless you have peanut butter and jelly, or macaroni and cheese, I've probably never had it." My voice breaks as I finish.

Sadly, I miss peanut butter and jelly sandwiches and macaroni and cheese. Just weeks ago, I wished for a life where I'd never have to eat those two things again. Today, I'd eat it every day for the rest of my life to have my mom back.

He stares at me, and it's hard not to see the pity in his eyes. I hate pity. My gaze falls to his neck where I watch his Adams apple rise slowly and then fall when he swallows. His lips part as if he's going to say something, but he refrains.

I inwardly cringe. "I'm sorry. I didn't mean to sound like such a bitch…"

"Don't apologize, Emilia," he says quietly. "Don't ever apologize for who you are." He turns his head, his brown eyes fixated on something in the living room. The silence is uncomfortable, and I hold my breath, waiting for him to say something. "Pizza. We'll order pizza. Everyone likes pizza, right?" He forces a small smile and the pity is gone, replaced by concern.

"Sure, pizza sounds great. I'll be in the room. Just let me know when it gets here." I make a hasty retreat. My feet slap against the tile floor, and I hear him sigh loudly as I disappear back into the safe confines of my room. I grab my notebook and sit on the oversized white chaise lounge. I smile at the remembrance of my mom giving me this notebook. She knew I loved to journal and scribble thoughts in a notebook, and for my birthday last year, she gave me this leather-bound notebook. I knew we couldn't afford it, but she told me how Mr. Wilson drove her to the dime store in town to help her look for a gift for me, and when she saw this, she knew she had to buy it for me.

Opening the leather cover, I thumb through the pages, but I find myself watching Alex through the open bedroom door where he still stands. He rakes his hands over his face and rubs his temples, clearly frustrated.

Turning back to my notebook, I continue jotting notes and building my plan. My to-do list is short and simple, but critical. First, find a job—something where I can make decent money, and quickly. Second, figure out where I'm going from here. Do I go back to Illinois, to the life I've always dreaded, but the only life I've known? Or do I go for a fresh start somewhere else? I've always wanted to live on the coast… near the ocean, even though I've never seen it.

Swallowing hard, I set my pen aside and flip the pages back to the beginning, running my fingers over the stars I sketched. Every time I see stars, I think of my mom. A lump forms in my throat as I think about her, about her life. I asked her one time why she didn't give me up for adoption. We both could've had a better life. Her answer was simple. "You were the brightest star in my darkest moment. Every wish, every dream, every hope I had that vanished was replaced with something better—you." We had nothing, yet I had everything with her love and support. I truly believe her depression was incurable, and I can only pray now that she's happier, wherever she is.

I swat at the tears and take a deep breath as I turn to the clear plastic sleeve in my notebook. Inside, it is a picture of my mom and me at my high school graduation. There are only a few memories in my life documented with photographs, but this is my favorite. The look of pure happiness on her face is something I'll never forget. I smile at the memories of that warm June day, her arm wrapped tightly around my waist, and her head snuggled just under my chin.

I tuck the photo back into the sleeve before I get too

emotional, and then I smile at this good memory of her—of us.

A phone ringing pulls me from my thoughts. Through the crack in the open door, I see Alex take his cell and disappear down the hall. I decide to take this opportunity to explore the kitchen I've been drooling over since I got here six hours ago. I open the fridge and peek inside. Its sleek glass shelves are lined with everything you'd expect to see in a fridge—soda, bottled water, condiments, and fresh fruits and vegetables. To the right of the refrigerator, I open the door to find a pantry that could double as a bedroom. It's huge and stocked with dry goods, cereals, pasta, grains, and more. Standing at the oversized kitchen island, I take in the beauty. I've never seen a house as beautiful as this one except for in magazines.

For half a second, I envision making dinners and baking in this kitchen before reality sets in and I remember that I'm a visitor in a stranger's house. I shake my head, expelling my foolish thoughts. Leaning my hip against the granite countertop on the kitchen island, I absorb the enormity and richness of this place. I love that it's an old building renovated and made modern—old mixed with new.

Feeling eyes on me, I turn to see Alex standing in the hallway on his phone. He's leaning against the wall, listening to whoever is speaking on the phone, but his focus is on me. Our eyes lock for a brief moment before I hear him mumble a few words and then hang up. For a few seconds, he watches me intently, and then slips back into his office.

What am I doing here? I got into a car with a beautiful stranger and let him take me home. I should be afraid, I should feel fear—but I'm drawn to the danger—attracted to the stranger.

A light knock at the door has me jumping away from the

kitchen island. My stomach begins to grumble at the near presence of food. I twist the deadbolt lock and turn the handle, opening the door just as Alex slams it shut, pressing me hard against the large wood door.

His firm stomach rests on my back. "Don't ever open this door without knowing who it is." He breathes heavily, the warm air of his breath brushing my ear.

When I register what just happened, I notice my heart racing. "I'm sorry, I thought it was the pizza…"

"It probably is. But, Emilia—you cannot open…" He pauses, lowering his voice to a whisper. "You can't just open the door." I lick my lips nervously as words evade me.

"I'm sorry," I murmur and duck underneath his arm. "I didn't know." I glance over my shoulder to see him peering through the peephole. His rigid body relaxes, and then he opens the door and pays for the pizza. I walk quietly back to the kitchen, finding a seat at one of the barstools at the island. My stomach clenches when I hear Alex shut the door. I keep my eyes down and study the swirl of the stone in the granite counter, trying to focus on anything other than my racing heart.

My stomach twists angrily in knots, and I can't tell if it's hunger pains or the flash of desire that overcame me when Alex had me pressed against his front door. His rigid muscles pressed against me, the light smell of his cologne, those tempting lips so close to mine. I disregard those thoughts and watch Alex intently. He sets the box on the counter, and immediately, the smell fills the kitchen. My stomach growls loudly, and Alex sets a glass plate down in front of me. "Help yourself," he says, opening the box.

With a shaky hand, I reach in, pull out a piece of pizza, and set it on my plate.

"Why're you shaking?" He frowns at me.

I shrug, too nervous to tell him he makes me nervous. Everything about him intimidates me.

"Do I scare you?" he asks me, drawing out the question slowly.

"No." My answer is soft and not reassuring.

He laughs through his nose and shakes his head. "I didn't mean to scare you. I'm sorry if I did."

"Maybe you did a little." I force a small smile. "Just tell me if there are things I shouldn't do. I feel awkward enough just being here."

"Don't."

"Don't what?" I stare at the slice of pizza, the cheese sliding off the crust onto the glass plate.

"Feel awkward about being here. I invited you. You're welcome to stay here as long as you need." He seems sincere enough, but every instinct tells me I shouldn't be here. I should never have accepted his invitation.

"Thank you, I really appreciate that, but I don't plan to stay for long." I pick up the large piece of pizza, blowing on it before I take a bite off the end.

"Can I ask you something without you getting upset?" He pushes away from the island and walks toward me. Only a small breakfast bar separates us. I set my pizza down and nod at him.

"Is everything you own in that room with you?"

I swallow hard and nod again; embarrassed, I feel myself blush.

"So, along with what you're wearing, you have two outfits hanging in the closet, your bag, a book, a notebook, and fifty dollars to your name?"

"Yes." Shameful, but true.

He stands quietly, his amber eyes holding mine, and his full lips pressed firmly together. I hold my breath, waiting for him to say something—but he never does, so I break the silence.

"Thanks for the pizza." I push my chair back, the legs squeaking against the tile floor.

He blinks twice before taking a step back. "You're not done eating. There's a whole pizza left."

"I'm not very hungry."

"Eat, Emilia." I can tell he's not taking no for an answer. He looks upset as he looks between the plate and back to me.

Sighing, I pull my chair back up to the counter and take another slice of pizza from the box, setting it next to the half-eaten piece on my plate. He tosses his crust into the trash and starts shuffling through drawers and cabinets, slamming them when he doesn't find what he's looking for.

I pick at my pizza, chewing on the crust slowly while watching him curiously. "What're you looking for?"

"Those metal pans. The long and flat kind. You know, the ones you make cookies on?" He holds his hands out to describe the size of the pan.

I smile and chuckle under my breath. "A cookie sheet?"

He blinks as if understanding is dawning. "Is that what they're called?"

I nod slowly. "Yeah. Try that tall, skinny cabinet next to your stove."

He hesitates for a moment, glancing over his shoulder at me before checking there. "I'll be damned." With a grin, he pulls out the shiny metal pan. "Did you know this was in there?"

I snort. "How would I know what's in your kitchen? Lucky guess."

I don't tell him that that's usually where the cookie sheets are. Taking another bite of warm pizza, I chew carefully as he leans against the kitchen island, watching me eat. I see a small smile pull at the corner of his lips when he sees me swallow my pizza as if he's satisfied with me. With a slight shake of his head, he sets the sheet pan on the island and pulls open the freezer drawer of his fancy refrigerator. It takes a minute, as if he doesn't know what's in his own freezer. Finally, he pulls out a cardboard box and sets it next to the pan.

I notice again how the immaculate the kitchen is, nothing on the counters except a complex-looking coffee maker that looks like it belongs in a coffee shop, and a hand towel next to the kitchen sink. Everything in this condo is neat, tidy, and has a place.

He looks up at me as I stand and carry my plate to the sink.

"Just leave the plate in the sink. My housekeeper will take care of it tomorrow."

Housekeeper? Holding in a begrudging sigh, I set the plate in the large porcelain sink. "You have a housekeeper? For what?"

The muscles in his tan arms tighten as he starts setting frozen dough balls on the pan. "She cleans, shops, and even cooks," he says, rearranging the little balls so they're perfectly spaced apart on the cookie sheet. Everything about Alex and his home is perfect, even the spacing of the dough balls on the cookie sheet. There's nothing out of place here.

Except for me.

"She basically keeps the house in order while I tend to my business." One ball rolls slightly out of place, and he painstakingly fixes it. "What are you thinking about?" he asks as I stare at his hands.

"Nothing." I squeeze my eyes shut for a moment. I feel so out of place here, and this is where Alex fits in so well. We're so different, yet I'm drawn to him.

He gives me a gentle smile. "One of these days, I'm going to get you to talk to me," he says, sliding the cookie sheet into the oven.

Days? I'm not planning on staying that long. But I don't say that. Instead, I give him, "You pretty much know everything about me." I run my fingers through my hair, something I catch myself doing frequently when I'm nervous.

"I seriously doubt that." He raises an eyebrow at me. Every time he looks at me, my heart races. There's something about him that I can't put my finger on, but my body reacts to him. Every look, every glance, I feel like he sees through me. He scares me and excites me all with one look. I'm intrigued and fearful all in the same breath.

I smile at his remark, but I don't respond, instead pulling away and heading back to the guest room. Slipping inside the cool room, I close the door and pull the long, sheer curtains open. I'm surprised when I realize what I thought were floor-to-ceiling windows is actually a sliding glass door that leads to a large patio. Stepping outside, the hot cement stings my bare feet as I tiptoe over to the plush outdoor furniture and sink into one of the oversized wicker chairs. The plush cushions swallow me, encasing me in warmth as I settle into the chair, thinking how peaceful it is out here.

This patio could double as a garden. There are planters that hold small trees, cacti flowers, and shrubs. A hummingbird flutters around a small feeder hanging from one of the trees, and I fixate on its little wings fluttering from blooming flower to blooming flower. A large stone fireplace sits in the center, outdoor couches surrounding it. I've never seen such wealth, such luxury. With that thought, the large French door swings open from the living room and Alex pokes his head out.

"What're you doing? It's a hundred and ten out here. Come inside; the dessert is ready."

"I'm not really a dessert eater, but thank you." I rest my feet on the edge of the chair and pull my knees tightly to my chest.

"She doesn't eat dessert," I hear him mumble to himself. He sighs, and the patio door closes.

Good. I need to think. I close my eyes and lean back in the chair as I soak in the warm afternoon sun.

A couple minutes later, I hear the doors slide open again, and Alex appears, juggling two bowls in his hands. "Here." He shoves one of the bowls at me with an annoyed tone. I want to ask him if he didn't hear me earlier when I said I didn't eat dessert, but instead, I accept the bowl with a gracious smile.

"Warm chocolate chip cookies with ice cream. It's my favorite," he says as he sits down in a matching chair across from me. I hold the glass bowl in my hand and watch as the vanilla ice cream starts to melt and pool around the warm cookies. Alex digs in, pulling up a heaping scoop of gooey cookie and ice cream. I find it hard to look away as he wraps his perfect lips around the spoon. The gold flecks in his eyes dance in the setting sun, and I'm mesmerized by how quickly he inhales bite after bite of his dessert.

I swallow hard when he catches me watching him, and I divert my eyes back to the bowl in my lap, which is now nothing more than cookies drowning in ice cream soup. I take a small bite, and then I set the spoon back in the bowl.

He looks at my uneaten dessert. "What's wrong?" His bowl is now empty and sitting on the iron table between us.

"Nothing. I'm just not really hungry." I feel bad wasting food, but my stomach twists nervously, and I just don't think I can eat it. I never ate a lot of sweets growing up, so now when I do, my stomach gets upset.

"Do you not like chocolate chip cookies?"

"I like chocolate chip cookies." I pause, remembering the times I'd make cookies with my mom. "They were more of a luxury at my house, though. My mom and I would make them on special occasions when we had the money to splurge. We didn't have them very often."

"My mom used to make the best chocolate chip cookies," Alex says quietly, leaning forward in his seat. He rests his elbows on his knees and laces his fingers together. "She would let me stir the chocolate chips into the dough, and my brother and I would always steal spoonfuls of dough. She'd get so mad because I'd eat half the dough before she even got a chance to make the cookies." He chuckles at the memory. "She's the reason I love warm cookies and ice cream." He nods toward his empty bowl.

That's a sweet memory. "Does she still make them for you?" I ask, trying to dig some information out of Alex.

His smile falters. "Nah, she's been gone a long time. Almost twenty years." Sitting back in his seat, his posture tenses. "Just my dad and me now, and let's just say he was never into baking." The comment is laced with sarcasm, but I detect anger as well.

"I loved baking," I whisper. "When I could."

"She loved baking too." Our eyes meet, and beyond the face

that could grace the covers of men's fashion magazines, the chiseled muscles and perfect hair, I see a world of sadness and hurt.

"How did she die?" I ask hesitantly, knowing better than to ask such a personal question.

He stares off into the dusk, avoiding my question. Embarrassed for being so nosy, I reach over and grab his bowl, heading toward the kitchen. Maybe if I do the cleanup, he'll forget I asked. Guiding the patio door open with my elbow, I juggle the glass bowls in my hands as I hear Alex mutter behind me, his voice strained with emotion.

"She was murdered."

chapter four

Emilia

I TOSS AND turn for hours. I've watched the minutes slowly change on the bedside clock while the bright moonlight peeks in through the sheer curtains. A million thoughts, a million questions, and a million unknown answers race through my mind as I stave off sleep. Sitting up, I toss my legs over the side of the bed, my feet hitting the floor. Traipsing across the room to the bathroom, I feel along the cool, tiled wall for a light switch.

When blinding light fills the room, I fling my hand up to cover my eyes. The white walls, the white tile, the white porcelain fixtures do nothing to ward off the brightness. I turn the knob on the bathtub faucet and begin filling the deep tub with warm water. I hope a bath will calm me. Standing in front of the full-length mirror, I slide my arms out from my bra and pull off my panties. My long hair hangs long in loose waves, and my skin looks ashen and gray. I look like death.

Ugh...

Climbing into the gigantic tub, I'm surprised my five-foot-nine frame can almost fully extend. My muscles begin to relax around the warm water, and I rest my head back on the edge of the tub. Soaking a washcloth in the warm water, I roll it and lay it over my eyes, inhaling deep breaths as my body begins to finally relax. I must've dozed because when I finally come to, the bath water is cool and goose bumps prick at my wrinkled skin. I was that tired. Pulling the plug on the drain, I turn on the water and start the shower.

Using the small bottle of body wash and shampoo that sit on the side of the tub, I quickly shampoo my hair and wash my body, stepping out onto the plush rug that sits outside the shower. Twisting my long hair into a towel on the top of my head, I find another to dry my body before wrapping it around me, securing it in place. I tug the towel from my head and run a comb through the tangles, letting my long hair hang loose to air dry over my shoulders.

Thirst has set in, and I glance between the alarm clock flashing three in the morning and the closed bedroom door. My bra and panties are in a pile on the bathroom floor, and I don't have any pajamas or a robe to throw on. *I'll be quick.*

Ensuring the towel is securely wrapped around me, I slowly pull the door open just a few inches. Peeking down the hall, I see no sign of Alex. The condo is dark. *I'll be really quick.* Slipping out the door and into the hall, I tiptoe to the kitchen, careful not to trip over any barstools.

Reaching into the fridge, I pull out a bottle of water and twist off the top, sipping the cool liquid. *Heaven.* As I head back to the bedroom, I stop in front of the pantry, debating. I should go back to my room, but I'm curious.

Quietly twisting the handle, I step inside and flip on the light, studying everything inside and making note of all the ingredients I'd need to make homemade chocolate chip cookie dough for Alex.

"Find what you're looking for?" His voice is soft, but it startles me.

"Shit!" I yelp, whipping around as the bottle of water tumbles from my hands.

A low chuckle slips from Alex's lips, and he reaches down to pick it up. "Are you always jumpy, Emilia?"

"Only when you keep surprising me," I breathe, pressing a hand to my heaving chest. "Why're you up?"

He quirks an inquiring eyebrow. "Better question is, why're *you* up?"

I blink momentarily, just now noticing that he's in the same pair of basketball shorts he had on earlier, but now he's shirtless. Jesus, his sculpted chest is perfect. I inhale sharply as I study every ridge, every curve. A few small tattoos mark his tanned skin, but the large crucifix over his heart is what catches my attention. The detail is incredible and the name "Emma" is etched below it. My breath hitches as my eyes travel from his chest down his firm stomach, to the fine sprinkling of dark hair just under his belly button.

"I couldn't sleep so I took a bath…" I realize now that I'm standing in his kitchen pantry in nothing but a bath towel. Embarrassed, I tuck in the top of the towel just a little tighter to make sure it's secure. "And then I came out here to get something to drink."

A smile tugs at the corner of his perfect lips. My heart races—and heat floods my body. He hands the water bottle back to me but doesn't immediately let go. "In my pantry?"

"No, I took the water from your fridge," I mumble, anxiety coursing through me. I move quickly, trying to get past him, but he grabs hold of my upper arms; his thumb's slowly swiping at my collarbone.

He's silent for a moment, then, "Are you hungry? I'll make you something to eat."

"No, I'm not hungry." I shake my head frantically.

"Then what're you doing in the pantry?" He cracks a devious smile at me.

I glance back at the stocked shelves. "I was just looking to see what you had. I'm sorry. I didn't mean to be nosy."

We stand, silently taking in each other's presence. Goosebumps form against my damp skin as the air conditioner blows cold air above us. Alex steps forward, pressing his warm hands onto my shoulders.

"You're still wet." He continues running the pads of his thumbs across my collarbone, swiping at the beads of water, and I swallow hard at the tender touch. "And you smell like me." He leans in closer, our noses nearly brushing as he deeply inhales the scent of his shampoo.

"I used what you had in the bathroom. I hope that's okay." That's why it was there, right? Maybe he expected me to have my own? My thoughts fluster me.

His touch sends tremors through my body as I stand cemented in place. His hand travels upward, and he finally rests his thumb in the hollow of my neck, my heart thrumming wildly in my chest. I can feel my pulse against his thumb, throbbing in time to my heartbeat. Alex can feel it too. A cocky grin stretches across his face. He knows what his touch is doing to me.

"Feel that," he whispers, his large hand tightening gently

around my throat. It's a firm, controlling, yet subtle grip.

I nod, inhaling sharply. Squeezing the bottle in my hand, I pull away from him and he lets go. Because whatever this is—if it's anything—I'm not ready for it. I won't be here long. In a few days' time, or less, I'll be gone, and I'll never see this guy again. *Never.*

As I'm rushing back to the guest room, I hear a soft "Goodnight, Emilia," and then a small laugh.

I WAKE UP tired, not sure if I really ever fell asleep. I was restless the remainder of the night with thoughts of Alex's hands on my neck and shoulders, his lips so close to mine—yet just out of reach. My feet kick at the white silk sheet that my legs are tangled in, and I pull the hair tie from the end of my long braid. Running my fingers through my hair from root to end, I loosen the braid so my hair falls into long waves.

With only three outfits to my name, I opt for the pair of cut-off jean shorts and a tank top. After a quick splash of water on my face, I brush my teeth and slide into my sandals before heading quietly into the kitchen. The condo is still, not a noise to be heard, and I hope to sneak out quickly in hopes of finding a store to pick up a few items with the fifty dollars I have left in my purse. Sunlight illuminates the space through the large skylights in the ceiling, and a lone envelope sits on the counter with my name scribbled across the front.

Glancing down the hallway, I notice the office is dark; no lights or signs of life anywhere. I pull the thick envelope from the counter and stare at my name. My finger slides under the flap and tears the envelope open. Inside is a handwritten note and cash.

Emilia,

I had some business to tend to this morning. Saul will take you anywhere you need to go and get you anything you need to make you more comfortable while you're here.

Alex.

P.S. Buy yourself some pajamas.

I remember Alex referring to the man I saw in the parking garage yesterday as Saul. He watched me tentatively and something inside me didn't settle well with his pensive look. Call it a sixth sense, but I don't trust him. I count out the cash inside and almost faint.

A thousand dollars?

I have to count it three times. Sure enough, there are ten crisp one-hundred-dollar bills. *Why would he do this for me?* I've never had a thousand dollars to my name, ever, let alone cash in my hand to spend any way I like. Except it's not my money. Anything I use, I will have to pay back. I was raised to never accept a handout. This is borrowed money. I take three one-hundred-dollar bills and put them in my purse, leaving the note and remaining cash on the counter.

Just outside the door, I find two sets of elevators. The far set I remember as the ones that we took from the parking garage yesterday, and I assume that's where Saul is. I notice cameras aimed at each elevator, as well as the door to Alex's condo. Hesitating, I push the call button on the set closest to me and make the quick decision that I don't need Saul to chauffeur me around. I'll take the city bus and find a store. My plans also include finding a public library to use the internet and searching for a job.

The elevator brings me to a small yet sophisticated lobby. A man seated at a small desk looks up at me as I approach him to ask for directions to the nearest store and a bus that'll get me there. The sign that sits on the desk in front of him reads *concierge*. Fred is his name, he tells me. His expression is hesitant, but he gives me the information that I need. And with a sticky note in hand, I leave.

A short light rail ride later, I'm standing inside the Phoenix public library. Armed with a new library card, I'm directed to a small room with rows of computers for public use. I spend the next two hours searching "help wanted" ads online and find few prospects. My one and only job with the town grocer doesn't qualify me for much. Shoving down my disappointment, I decide I'll come back tomorrow to look again and type up a resume.

Checking my Google email, I find nothing. Not a single message. As pathetic as that is, it's not too surprising. My few friends at home were my coworkers, and we only saw each other at work. We exchanged emails before I left, but I've only been gone a couple days. Not enough time for them to miss me yet—if ever.

The rest of my afternoon is spent wandering the aisles of a local Target. I've never been inside a Target before, and I'm enamored. This is the holy grail of shopping experiences. Anything a person could ever need or want is in this store. I carry a small shopping basket and pick up some shampoo, conditioner, deodorant, a bottle of body wash, and a small pack of razors. I pick out clothes, pajamas, and a couple pairs of shoes. I also am sure to grab some new bras and panties. I've never had the luxury of purchasing anything I wanted. It was necessities only. I should feel guilty spending Alex's money, but I promise myself I'll pay him back every penny. Besides, I need clothes if I'm going to land a decent job.

Happy with my purchases, I ride the light rail back toward downtown. The city zips by as the train winds through the busy downtown streets. A sea of people surround me, sitting and standing—professionals, students, and even a handful of homeless people—I assume by their appearance. But I love that all walks of life are together here, in this small space. It makes me smile.

As I walk back toward Alex's condo, I find a small coffee shop tucked into the side of one of the tower office buildings. From the sidewalk, I peer through the large glass window. It's small and quaint with plush leather couches and small two-person bistro tables. Even though it's boiling outside, I suddenly find myself craving a coffee, so I push through the glass door and weave around the tables to the counter. I splurge and order an iced coffee, inhaling the bittersweet aroma of coffee beans and fresh baked pastries while taking in the college students on laptops and businessmen and women laughing and talking. As I wait for the barista to make my drink, I notice the small "help wanted" sign taped to the counter.

Whipping back to the rugged, yet extremely good-looking man, I ask, "Are you hiring?" I nod toward the help wanted sign.

"We are!" he says delightedly. "Are you looking for work?"

I peel the paper wrapper off the straw and shove it in the plastic coffee cup while I juggle the Target bags on my left arm. "I am. I just got into town a couple of days ago," I say excitedly. A momentary sense of hope flashes through me that maybe, just maybe, I could get a job here.

"Ah, back to school. Tis' the season." He chuckles and bends down behind the counter, handing me a paper application. "Here. Fill this out and bring it back tomorrow. Ask for Megan; she's the owner. We're short-handed, so I know she's looking to fill the position as soon as possible. I'm Jax," he adds with a polite smile.

"Emilia." I offer my own smile. This is the most hope I've felt since I arrived here. "Nice to meet you, Jax."

"Nice to meet you too."

Juggling the plastic shopping bags and the cold cup of coffee, I push open the door to the lobby of Alex's brown brick building. The concierge jumps up from his stool and shoots me a concerned look as he rushes toward me.

"Hi," I offer as I move past him toward the elevator.

"Miss?" He reaches for the phone on his desk. "Mr. Estrada has been looking for you, and he's not happy. You didn't tell me you were staying with *him*." He emphasizes the word, his eyes oddly sympathetic, but his expression changes quickly when he presses the receiver of his desk phone to his ear. "She's arrived and is on her way up."

"I didn't know I was supposed to tell you," I respond innocently as he calls the elevator and waits with me, nervously tapping his hand against the side of his thigh.

"Mr. Estrada is very careful with his business," he responds hesitantly.

"I'm not his business," I reply, confused... and curious. *His business. What does that mean?*

The old man takes a deep breath, then shoves me gently into

the elevator, sending me on my way. The ride up to the tenth floor seems to take an eternity. I glance at the bags, wondering why he'd be so upset. After a moment, I start to feel guilty. I used his money today. I shouldn't have. Now I owe him. This could be bad. My stomach flips as the elevator halts and the doors open.

Saul from the parking garage is waiting for me as I step out. His eyebrows are furrowed and his thick arms are folded across his chest. I'm immediately intimidated by Saul. Even though he's not as tall as Alex, standing only a few inches taller than me, he looks as though he could be a bodybuilder. With bulging muscles poking out from underneath his black polo shirt, he steps aside to let me move past him. His dark eyes narrow in annoyance as he takes me in from head to toe.

"Excuse me," I say as I try to step around him.

"Where the fuck were you?" he growls at me.

I freeze in place. This is the first time he's ever spoken to me and his tone is bitter—angry. In shock, I try to piece together what I could've done. I've taken care of myself all of my life, so I don't understand how an outing to the library and store is causing this much anger.

"I went to the library and…"

"Emilia." My heart stops at the sound Alex's voice. It's commanding, yet concerned.

I turn to find him with one hand on the door, holding it open, and the other against the frame. His tanned fingers flex and grip the frame, and I can see the veins bulging in his forearm.

What the hell is going on?

"You went to the fucking library," Saul sneers. "How cute. Did you check out a book?"

I swallow hard against my dry throat and feel the tears

prick at the back of my eyes.

"That'll be enough," Alex barks at Saul. "Do not talk to her like that ever again. Do you understand?" The air is fraught with tension as the two men stare at each other. "I said, do you understand?"

Both men are aggressive in their posture, an entire unspoken showdown until they eventually nod, and Saul concedes, retreating into a stairwell next to the elevator.

I stand frozen, looking at Alex. Finally, his arms fall from their locked position on the door, and he steps back into the condo. But as I walk slowly toward him, he steps in front of me. "Don't ever leave here again without Saul. Do you understand?" I'm a grown woman. Twenty-one years old. I don't need a babysitter. I don't need protection—but I listen to Alex's concern and reasoning.

Yet something stirs inside me as I try to decipher what I did wrong. "No, I don't understand." My entire body trembles as I speak. "And if Saul is a condition, I can't stay here. I won't stay here." I drop the bags at his feet and turn around, heading back toward the elevator. As I reach forward to press the call button, a hand wraps around my wrist, tugging me away from the elevator.

"Let me go." I'm embarrassed at how fragile my voice sounds.

Slowly, he shakes his head before his full lips part and a vulnerable plea escapes. "I can't."

chapter five
Alex

I GLANCE AT the Rolex on my wrist and then back to the closed bedroom door where Emilia is hiding. The Target bags still sit in a pile just inside the front door, and her iced coffee is on the counter, becoming room temperature as the minutes pass. I watch the ice slowly dissolve and the condensation roll down the side of the plastic cup, pooling on the granite counter that it sits on. I decide to wait another thirty minutes or so before I force her out here to eat dinner. Rosa, my housekeeper, made lasagna and it's almost done. I lean against the island as I sip on a beer, my eyes never leaving her door. I'm not a patient man, but I could tell she needed time to herself to calm down, and quite frankly, I needed to figure out what to say to her. What to tell her—or rather, what I *can* tell her—about me. Finally, I spot the nickel door handle begin to slowly turn, and Emilia peeks her head out.

"You've been crying." My fingers grip the edge of the counter, rooting me in place. I want so badly to pull her into my arms and comfort her. Her sad, puffy eyes find mine, and I feel guilty.

She nods slowly. "I don't understand—"

"You wouldn't," I cut her off.

She exhales loudly in frustration. "Then explain it to me."

"I can't." I run my fingers through my short hair in frustration.

"You won't," she argues.

I laugh, setting the beer bottle on the kitchen counter in frustration. It clanks against the granite, echoing in the open space. She's pushing me, and while it angers me, it's that spark in her eye that excites me.

"You're intuitive, Emilia."

"You're evasive." She crosses her arms stubbornly over her chest.

"Because I have to be," I insist. She doesn't understand that this has to do with her safety. But I don't tell her that. It'd scare her away.

She approaches and plants herself directly in front of me, her pink lips pursed, eyes narrowed. She's angry. The strap of her tank top hangs off one shoulder, and it takes every ounce of self-control not to reach out and brush my fingers across her soft skin. She tightens the cross of her arms, lifting her breasts higher, and I can't help but wonder what they'd feel like in my hands.

"Why?" she asks.

"Because of who I am."

Her expression is simultaneously hurt, curious, and a little scared. "Who are you?"

I ask myself that same damn question all the time. *Who am I?*

I pause, searching for the words to describe exactly who I

am. I knew she'd ask me. And for the last thirty minutes, I've sat here and wondered what I would tell her. I should tell her the truth. I'm evil. I run my father's business. We smuggle drugs, guns, and people across the U.S./Mexican border.

Instead, I offer her lies. "I'm an international businessman."

She cocks her head and raises her eyebrows. "Okaaaay... and?"

"My business is confidential. That's all I can tell you. It's for your own safety," I finally add.

"Safety from what?" I can see her need to know in those eyes, those hazel eyes. "What is so dangerous about what you do?"

I let out a long and tired sigh. "Leave it alone, Emilia. You're safe. You'll always be safe with me." Another lie.

"I just don't understand. Why would I be in danger? You and I are basically strangers."

I tap my fingers against the granite, choosing my words wisely. "There are some people who will do anything to get to me, or hurt anyone who has access to me." *Now please drop it.*

Her eyes grow wide as she absorbs this.

Time to move on. "Let's eat dinner, and we'll figure this out later, okay?" The lasagna has been ready for a few minutes, and the house smells of the fresh baked pasta and garlic bread.

We stand in silence, her expression still full of questions.

"C'mon." I slide my hand into hers and guide her to the dining room off the other side of the kitchen.

"I didn't know this was here." Her eyes dance around the room, taking in the expensive imported paintings on the wall. My father spent a small fortune for those in Mexico City. I pull out a chair at the large, round table built just for this room, and she takes a seat.

"That's because you've barely left your room." I smirk at her.

She raises one eyebrow at me. I love her expressions. She can tell a story with just the expressions on her face. "Do you really want a stranger snooping around your house? I mean, you freaked out when you found me in your pantry." She sets her cotton napkin in her lap.

"You're not a stranger, and I didn't freak out. I was curious. You were in my pantry... in the middle of the night... wearing nothing but a towel." She drops her eyes to her hands, which are folded in her lap, and I add warmly, "I'll give you the official tour after dinner."

I bow my head and whisper a quiet prayer, thanking the Lord for the food before us, for protecting me... and for bringing me Emilia. And then we eat. For being Mexican, Rosa makes the most amazing lasagna I've ever tasted.

I eat while Emilia mostly pushes food around her plate. "Not hungry?" I ask her. It bothers me that she doesn't eat when I know she hasn't had a good meal in God only knows how long.

She shrugs. "It's actually really good."

"Then eat it."

She picks at her garlic bread with her delicate fingers. "I might've found a job," she says quietly, popping in a small piece of garlic bread. She takes one bite of lasagna, then sets her fork on her plate and pushes it away as if she's done.

"That was fast. Where?" I want to scream at her to finish her food, but her eyes dance with excitement, so I'll let this meal pass without badgering her.

She swallows and wipes her mouth. "That little coffee shop

in the building next door. Café Au Lait."

I nod. At least it's close. I can easily have one of my guys watch her. Discreetly, so she doesn't know, of course. And this solves the Saul problem, at least while she's at work. I can't help but smile.

"I have to turn in the application tomorrow," she says with her own smile.

I'll make sure she gets the job.

"Alex." She hesitates. "I don't know how much money I'll make at a coffee shop, but I'll pay back every penny of what you lent me and rent as well."

"I'm not worried about the money." I set the fork down in annoyance that she's still worried about money and paying back.

"Well, I am," she says, bothered. "I've never taken a handout, and I won't start now."

"It's not a handout," I make clear.

"Then a loan. I'll pay you back." She's persistent, I'll give her that.

"Okay," I relent finally, adding, "But I don't charge interest on loans."

She shakes her head and laughs before going quiet again. "About Saul," she says. "I don't like him."

"You don't have to like him. He's there for protection only, not to be your friend."

"I don't trust him either." She drops her eyes to the table when she tells me.

"I do." I have to because my father does and I have very few people I trust.

She lets out an aggravated sigh.

Almost as if the words fall out of my mouth, I say, "If you

stay, I'll find someone else for you, Emilia." *If* she stays… Now isn't that a prospect? I hadn't really thought about her leaving until now. What if she tries to leave? My heart sinks at the thought of her leaving and that irritates me.

Something flickers in her eyes, a fire pulling me from my thoughts of her leaving. Stubbornness maybe? But it looks like something else. "First of all, I don't need anyone to protect me."

"It's not open for negotiation. I'll find someone else for you."

She narrows her eyes, cracking a small, suspicious smile. "Seems like a lot of work to keep a roommate. Maybe you're better off without me here."

Impossible, I think to myself. I have never felt more comfortable around someone, and I've never enjoyed spending my time with someone like I do Emilia. "It's no problem at all," I say without hesitation. "I like having you here."

"I like being here," she admits shyly.

I can't help the grin that spreads across my face. "C'mon. Let me show you the rest of the place." I push my plate to the center of the table next to hers.

I stand up, pulling out her chair for her, and she follows me out. Reaching over, I pull her hand into mine, and without hesitation, she lets me. Down the long hallway, I point out each room as we pass.

"My office is here on the left." The glass French doors allow her to see inside. My oversized desk sits in the center of the room and computer monitors line the edge of the desk.

"That's a lot of computers," she remarks.

"Just monitors. One is my computer, and two are security feeds."

"Security?" Fear flashes through her eyes.

I point to the obscure cameras outside each room. Emilia tenses as she sees the first one.

Trying to lighten the mood, I squeeze her hand and joke, "I have better security here than Fort Knox." Sadly, it's practically true.

Her eyes dance from door to door down the hallway, and her head turns to take in all the small cameras tucked carefully into corners. What she doesn't see are the ones hidden meticulously behind paintings, artwork, and plants. This entire house is under twenty-four/seven surveillance.

"Are they everywhere?"

"Mostly. Not in bathrooms, not in your bedroom. But in the public areas and outside, yes."

She nods. "For your protection," she mumbles quietly.

"And yours."

She shakes her head at my comment, and I squeeze her hand again, tugging her gently toward the open room on the right. "Game room," I say.

She laughs. "You have a room for games?"

"Over the top?" I ask.

"Little bit." She rolls her eyes and lets go of my hand as she begins to wander, running her hand over the felt of the large pool table in the center of the room. An enormous flat screen TV hangs from the main wall and an oversized plush couch sits in front of it.

"Where I watch football." I shrug as she throws herself on the couch and stretches out.

"Are those autographed?" She jumps up from the couch and pads over to the wall full of signed photographs of professional athletes.

"Yeah."

"Jesus, Alex. These must be worth a small fortune."

I shrug it off and move to the other side of the room. "And this is the bar." I slide behind the long, wooden bar. The wall behind it is mirrored and stacked with liquor just like you'd find in a neighborhood bar.

"Holy shit," she mumbles. And again, I'm reminded of the extravagance of my life.

I pull a beer from the small fridge. "Want anything?" I ask as I use a bottle opener to remove the cap from my beer.

She blinks up at the wall of alcohol. "I've only drunk twice in my life. Do you have anything fruity?"

I chuckle quietly. "I have wine. Pinot Grigio is pretty light and fruity."

"Sounds perfect." A look of shy pleasure crosses her face as she spreads her slender arms over the bar. "A glass of Pinot Grigio, please."

I nod and pull out an expensive bottle from the wine cooler built into the bar. I'll keep the price to myself. I uncork the wine and let it sit for a few minutes while Emilia walks every inch of the game room and takes in every picture, every detail.

"Do you play darts?" She runs her fingertips across the cork dartboard affixed to the far wall.

"Sometimes. I like pool better." I nod to the pool table as I pour a small amount of wine into a glass and swirl it around.

She watches me... studies me as I walk across the room to meet her with the wine. "I've never played pool," she admits. "But it looks easy enough."

"It takes skill... a good eye. I'll teach you sometime." I've only played pool once in this house since I've lived here. Emilia is right. Everything is extravagant and over the top.

She takes a sip of her wine and leans against the side of the pool table. "I'd like that."

So would I. I could teach her how to hold a stick, how to aim for the one ball you want, how to shoot in a way that you never miss a pocket. I imagine the feel of her soft body pressed up against me as I lean over her, my nose pressed into her hair, my lips skimming the top of her ear.

"What else do I need to see?" She ambles toward the hallway, cutting off my impure thoughts.

I clear my throat, regaining control. "Down the hall is the laundry room. But Rosa will do your laundry. Just leave it in your room."

She pulls her head back as if that idea is preposterous. "I can do my own laundry."

Of course this girl has never been spoiled before. I aim to change that. I keep my voice light. "That's why I have Rosa. If she doesn't have work to do, I'll have to let her go." I wink at her. "You don't want me to fire Rosa, do you?" She narrows her eyes at me and rolls them again. I laugh at her. "And the end of the hall on the right is the gym, and on the left is my room." I pause, but Emilia keeps walking. She twists the handle and pushes my bedroom door open, entering without hesitation. I follow closely behind her.

"Holy mother of..." She presses her hands over her mouth in shock.

"It's not that outrageous," I say somewhat defensively.

"Are you kidding me? Are you freaking kidding me?" she bellows. "There's a waterfall in your room."

I frown. "It's not a waterfall; it's a water wall," I correct her.

She laughs. "A water wall. Excuse *me*."

I've never been embarrassed of my wealth, but having Emilia point out every over-the-top opulence has me feeling guilty.

"We didn't have running water in our trailer sometimes, and here you have a *wall* of it!"

I swallow hard as she points out the absurdity of the large piece of glass that separates the bedroom from the bathroom. Water runs down the glass and creates a privacy barrier between the two rooms. I swallow hard as her reality weighs on me. She has a point. But I love my water wall. It's soothing, helps me calm my racing mind and sleep.

She stands in front of it, closing her eyes as she listens. It's beautiful. *She's beautiful.* "I love the sound of water. Like a creek or a river. It's naturally relaxing."

I copy her, closing my own eyes and simply listening to sound of the water trickling down the glass and hitting the smooth river rocks at the bottom.

Then I startle when she shrieks, "And this bed! I've never seen a bed this big. What size is this?"

"Custom," I mumble and run my hand over my face.

"No shit," she says. "Look!" She sets her glass of wine on the nightstand. "If I reach my arms and legs out, there's still at least a foot on every side."

She lies down on the bed and stretches out just as she's describing. My cock twitches as I look at her sprawled out on my bed. Her short jean shorts barely cover the most private areas, and her long legs are spread wide. Her breasts rise and fall with each breath, and her long hair is splayed across the light gray bedding. Fuck, if I thought she was beautiful before, that was nothing in comparison to this image, right now.

She giggles and sits up. "I bet your girlfriend loves this." She reaches for her glass of wine and presses it against her plump bottom lip. I want to taste those lips. The desire is almost too much that I have to clench my hands into fists at my sides. We need to get out of my bedroom.

She tilts her head back and swallows another sip of wine, the soft flesh of her neck calling me. Fuck me, I want to taste that too. I want to taste all of her.

My entire body is heating, and I take three breaths to cool down when I finally reply, "I don't have a girlfriend."

"Why not?" She looks confused, as if someone like me would never be without a girlfriend.

I shrug. "Hasn't been a priority."

"Huh." She swings her legs over the edge of the mattress and slides off, carrying her glass of wine with her across the bedroom.

Thank the fucking Lord.

But then she heads straight for the only sacred place in my room, the chest of drawers that holds everything worth anything to me. "Who's this?" she asks, pointing to one of the picture frames along the top.

"My dad." I exhale loudly. *Can we leave now?*

She doesn't say anything, but studies the picture for a few moments before setting it down and picking up another one.

"Is this her?" She finds the one picture I keep of my mom. The picture of how I want to remember her—her smiling face, eyes full of love. Not the one of her lying on the bathroom floor, her skull littered with bullet holes.

I shake off the memory. "It is," I say quietly.

"She's... beautiful."

"She was." I nod in agreement. This picture represents the only good I ever had in my life. Life was good when my mom was alive. She knew how to make the bad good. I swallow hard.

"How old was she here? She looks so young."

"About twenty-five in that picture," I say, taking the frame from Emilia's hands. "I think I was five when this was taken. She had us very young."

"Who's 'us'?" she asks softly.

I pull another picture frame from the top of the chest and hand it to her. It's a family picture of my dad, my mom, my brother, and me.

"You have a brother?" she whispers.

"Had," I say bitterly. "We were twins."

"Did he die too?" Instant regret fills her eyes. "I'm sorry; I shouldn't have asked that."

"It's okay. He's not dead, but… he's no longer a part of our family. He hasn't been since we were seven. So he's dead to me."

"Jesus," she hisses and sucks in a breath. "So you don't talk to him?"

I actually laugh out loud. "Uh, no."

"Do you know where he lives?"

"I do."

"Maybe you should—"

I cut her off. "Let it go, Emilia." My voice is firm but gentle. She needs to know I'm not willing to discuss it. "The past is in the past. It's dead—he's dead to our family. Leave it there."

Emilia sets the frame back on the chest before turning to me. "You know what I don't understand? I would do anything to have a family. To have *one* person that loved me, and you… you write off a brother you haven't seen since you were seven."

My jaw hardens. "Emilia, it's a very complicated story—of which I'm not about to go into detail. Just know that it's what's best. For my family and for him."

"You have no idea what it's like to be alone, do you? To have no one?" Her eyes fill with sadness, and her words strike me.

I've always had my father and our cartel "family," although they're not blood related. "No, I don't know what that's like."

Her eyes sparkle with the slightest hint of tears, but her voice doesn't waver. "Let me fill you in, Alex. It's the worst feeling in the world. To have not one person I'm able to call or depend on. I could die tomorrow and who would care? No one. I have no one to celebrate birthdays with, or holidays, or call when something exciting happens. It's just me. I've never felt so lost in a world full of so many people. I would kill to have a brother— hell, I'd kill to have one person love me—care for me." Even though her words seem hopeless, there is strength behind them, behind that sadness, and passion behind that loneliness.

She stands close enough that I can smell the sweet wine on her breath, and I feel her vulnerability as her lower lip trembles. Before I use caution and think, I pull her to me and capture those lips with my own. I expect her to resist, but she doesn't. Instead, she lets her head fall back as I claim her.

With just one kiss, I know I'll never have enough of her. "I care, Emilia."

chapter six

Emilia

I RAN. I pulled away from Alex, and I ran.

Buried under my down comforter, I wrestle with what that kiss meant.

It was soft.

It was hungry.

It was sweet.

It was needy.

It was caring.

But most of all… it was claiming.

I let him kiss me, and I kissed him back. I can still taste him on my tongue, a combination of mint and beer. I can still feel his soft lips roaming while his firm hands held me in place just before I ran.

Why did I run?

Shit.

Kicking off the covers, I stumble out of bed and my feet hit the floor. The moonlight is peeking through the sheer curtains, casting just enough of a glow that I don't need a light. I catch a shadowed glimpse of myself in the mirror and curse under my breath for not buying a robe today. My very short pair of white satin sleep shorts and a matching spaghetti strap camisole leave little to the imagination.

I open the bedroom door and traipse down the hallway, knowing very well that the security cameras can see me. I find Alex sitting at his desk in his office. His face is buried in his hands, his elbows resting on the glass desk. I stand for a moment and watch him. The sharp lines of his jaw, his perfect nose. Everything about this man is perfection. I jump when the large clock on the wall sounds out, telling me that it's three in the morning. Alex is in his dark athletic shorts and T-shirt again, his hair a tousled mess.

"Alex," I say quietly as not to startle him. He doesn't move. Moving closer, I say his name again. He jumps, and I freeze. "I didn't mean to scare you."

His eyes are bloodshot as they focus on me. I catch a glimpse of the screen and see the security feeds are up, as well as two other screens. One screen shows an email account and the other an online banking session that has timed out.

"Come on. You need to go to bed." I reach for his hand, and he takes mine. I tug gently on his arm. He leans forward and shuts off the monitors that display information other than the security feed. In the hall, I let him go, nudging him toward his room.

"Goodnight, Alex," I whisper as I make a right turn back to my room, but his hand catches my wrist, stopping me.

"Why did you run away from me earlier?" He sounds hurt and his eyes search mine for answers.

It's the question I've replayed in my head over and over. I

hesitate answering him—my answer embarrassing even me.

"Why?" he presses.

"I don't need pity kisses. You felt sorry for me. I could see it in your eyes. Don't feel sorry for me." My voice is tense, clipped.

Before I can register what's happening, he has me pressed against the wall in the hallway, his lips on mine again. This time, they're needy—hungry.

"Alex." I gasp for air as his lips trace my jawline and down my neck. His taut stomach presses against me and holds me firmly against the wall. Suddenly, he stops and pulls away, his fingers still tangled in my hair. His dark eyes search mine as I try to regain my composure.

"Did that feel like pity?" He licks his bottom lip, tucking it between his teeth.

My mind moves a million miles an hour, but all I see in slow motion is that tongue as it swipes his lower lip.

"Answer me," he pleads, squeezing my shoulders. "Did that feel like pity?"

I shake my head, and a muffled response slips from my lips. "No."

For just a moment, he hesitates before he reaches out to me. "Come with me." He takes my hand, moving quickly down the hallway and into his bedroom. His room is noticeably darker than mine. I can make out the water wall, but everything else is almost pitch black. I hear him pulling the decorative pillows off his bed and tossing them to the floor before he releases my hand and pulls the comforter back on his bed.

"Get in." It's not a question or a suggestion; it's a demand.

I hesitate again and contemplate running for the second time tonight, but something inside me stirs. That fire that I have been feeling in my belly and the intense, yet foreign emotions I feel for Alex have me throwing caution to the wind and going with it. I step around him, sliding in. My skin and my satin pajamas glide across the cool silk sheets as I settle in. My heart races as I hear him round the bed, discarding his T-shirt and shorts before settling in next to me.

His arm wraps around my waist, pulling me closer to him, and I feel all of him—all six foot three of firm, naked male. "Tell me not to touch you, Emilia, and I won't," he whispers as he takes my lips again and I let him. I let him show me what he's feeling, since he won't tell me. I hum against his mouth, feeling the intensity of his kisses—soft, yet controlling. He rolls me onto my back, his large hand wrapping around my neck as he positions himself on top of me. His forefinger rubs small circles in the hollow of my neck until his lips make their way there. He kisses me tenderly and bites gently at the skin.

"This is my favorite place on you," he breathes against that shallow spot. My body relaxes and I relinquish any self-control that I believed I had. I'm his.

His hands push the slim satin straps of the camisole off my shoulders, and the loose top slinks its way down. The globes of my breasts peek out from the top of the white satin top, and he drops light kisses down my neck and over each shoulder blade while his fingers rub my taut nipples through the thin satin. I moan and he takes that as an invitation. With a fast tug, he pulls the top down further, freeing both breasts. He inhales sharply as he takes both into his palms. He's settled between my legs, and I can feel his warm, rock-hard length pressing against my inner thigh. The loose satin shorts provide essentially no barrier between us.

Placing his warm mouth over my right breast, his tongue swirls circles over the nipple until he finally pulls the tight bud into his mouth. His teeth gently nip at the sensitive skin, and I can feel myself coming undone beneath him. My hips rise when he repeats the same action to my left breast, and his cock hardens even more against me.

"Tell me to stop," he mumbles again between soft bites to my breast.

"No," I pant, shaking my head. I need him—I need to feel something, and maybe this is wrong. I'll most likely regret this in the morning. But right now, this is what I need.

"Say it again, Em. Do you want me to stop?" I love that he calls me Em, like I belong to him.

"No." My voice breaks. "Don't stop."

In one swift move, he rips the camisole from my chest and pulls himself off of me. Grabbing the waistband of my pajama shorts, he pulls them down before tossing them aside on the floor. I lie powerless beneath him. His eyes roam freely over me, studying every curve, every limb. Leaning forward, he takes a finger and trails it from my belly button down, pressing it against my opening. My legs fall open and the slick entrance is a sure sign that I'm ready for him.

"Are you on the pill?" he asks. "I'm clean."

"No, but I'm clean too."

He leans over and pulls a condom from the nightstand. "You'll have to take care of that. I want to feel you without one of these," he says, ripping the foil wrapper. Tossing it aside, he rolls the condom down his long shaft. He's an expert in everything he does. He's quick and efficient and takes control, positioning the head of his cock at my entrance. He stares directly into my eyes as he pushes in, filling me. I gasp at the intrusion and hold my breath, a mixture of pleasure and pain. A good pain. My hands grip his biceps as he fills me completely.

"So fucking good, Emilia. So warm and wet," he murmurs against my lips, withdrawing himself almost completely. I panic as I feel him leave me, but with a heady thrust, he forces his way back inside, pounding against my insides.

"Oh God," I breathe as he does this again and again.

He hooks my long legs over his arms, opening me wide to him as his thrusts become faster. I've had sex before, but this is nothing like I've ever experienced. Alex is a master, and he knows how to work my body. My hands grasp and scratch the skin of his back as he fills me again and again.

"Alex," I muster between breaths. I can feel my orgasm building, but I'm not ready to let go yet. I want this to last—I want him inside me all night. No other man has made me feel cherished, worshipped, and cared for before. I've only been with boys, not men, and Alex is a man.

"Stop," I gasp as he slams into me, then comes to an abrupt stop.

"What's wrong? Did I hurt you?" His face is concerned, caring.

My head falls back and my eyes close. "No. I'm just not ready yet."

"Oh no, you don't get to call the shots. I do." He picks up his pace again, this time, his finger swirling around my swollen clit. "I will make you come when I want to, how I want to, and as many times as I want to. Do you understand?" I've always been in control of everything. For now, I relinquish that control to Alex. He's demanding, but careful—forceful, but gentle. As he takes control of me, I fear it's not just my body I'm handing over to him—it's my heart.

I nod, too many feelings swirling through me to properly answer. He pulls my legs up over his shoulders one at a time, giving him better access as he thrusts deeper, filling every inch of me. I can feel the pressure deep inside me—not painful, but full.

My hands grasp his forearms, and he presses his forehead against mine. We're a combination of deep breaths and groans, our eyes never leaving or wavering from one another. My body begins to shudder, and my head falls back as my orgasm takes over.

"Look at me. I want to see you when you come," he says, a smug smile tugging at his lips. He pulls my legs off his shoulders as my body comes down from its high. I tremble as I wrap my arms around his neck and press my lips to his.

"God, you're beautiful when you come."

I inhale sharply as I catch my breath.

His pace quickens, and I wrap my legs tightly around him. Our bodies are a tangled mess of sweaty arms and legs.

"Come for me now," I tell him.

With his breathing heavy, he slams into me one last time, and I feel his cock throbbing against my inner walls. He rests his head on the pillow, our cheeks touching as I hear him try to catch his breath. I trail my fingers up and down his spine and feel goose bumps prick at the soft skin of his back.

"I'm not done with you yet, Emilia," I hear him whisper into the pillow, and I can't help but smile.

I WAKE SUDDENLY, disoriented in a dark room. I struggle to sit up when I realize a warm body is wrapped around mine.

"What's wrong?" Alex mumbles into the back of my head. I relive every moment of last night in my head. His hand rubs small circles across my belly and that fire is back. Desire pools deep inside and I want more of him—all of him.

"Time to get up."

"Lie here with me." His voice is groggy as I twist around to face him. He drapes his arm over my side and pulls me closer, our naked bodies touching. "I like sleeping next to you," he mumbles, "and with you."

I sigh lightly but don't shrug out of his embrace. I lie face to face with Alex, listening to the slight wheeze of his lungs. I can feel his warm breath on my neck and, for a moment, I feel happiness. Within minutes, he's fast asleep again, his breathing steady, so I make my escape. I slide his arm off of me and sneak out of bed, making no attempt to find my torn pajama top. I shrug on my bottoms before tiptoeing through to the door.

I move quickly down the hallway, back to the comfort of the guest room. Then, just as I near the kitchen, I see a woman with her back to me. I have two options: turn around and head back to Alex's room or continue to mine and hopefully not get caught shirtless. I decide on the latter. I'm within steps of my doorway when I hear a loud voice shriek and a flurry of Spanish words.

My right arm covers my bare breasts as I glance over my shoulder. "I'm so sorry," I whisper. "My name is Emilia."

"Emilia, sí." She grimaces. "I'm Rosa." Her accent is thick, but her English is good. Rosa is short compared to me. Her hair is pulled back into a bun, with a sprinkling of gray at each temple, and her skin is light brown and flawless. She is heavyset and looks to be around fifty or so.

"I was just…" *What exactly do I tell her?*

"No need to explain yourself, *mija*." She attempts an awkward smile. "What can I make you for breakfast?" Her brown eyes twinkle and her smile is big, comforting. Her nonchalance to my naked body has me wondering if this happens often, Alex and naked women. I dismiss the thoughts and use both arms to shield my naked chest as I back slowly into my room. "Nothing, thank you. I'll grab something once I get ready."

"Mr. Estrada told me you'd be stubborn." She shakes her head and chuckles. "Let me cook for you."

I smile, happy that Alex has mentioned me. "Scrambled eggs would be nice. Thank you."

"Scrambled eggs it is. Now go get some clothes on, child." She laughs as she turns around and pulls a pan out from a cabinet. I slip further into the room and pull a new outfit out of the closet and lay it across the freshly made bed that Rosa must've made.

I shower and dress, leaving my hair to air dry. Grabbing the paper application for Café Au Lait, I head to the kitchen and sit at the island to fill it out. After reading through the questions, I decide to leave out the parts I don't have answers to. I don't even know my address, and I've never had a phone number.

Rosa sets a plate of eggs, bacon, and toast in front of me, along with a large glass of orange juice and a small bowl of oatmeal.

My eyes bulge at the amount of food. "Rosa, I'll never eat all this!"

"Orders from Mr. Estrada. He wants you to eat." She gives me a no-nonsense look. When I give her my own grimace, her expression turns sympathetic. "Eat what you can, dear."

She taps my hand with hers before scurrying over to the sink to wash the dishes. While I eat, I finish the application and set it aside. I eat most of my breakfast and am sipping my orange juice when Alex appears in the kitchen. He's wearing the athletic shorts from last night and no shirt.

Oh my God. That chest.

"Shirtless, Mr. Estrada," Rosa says. "Seems like a common theme this morning." She chuckles.

Alex glances at me, and I blush.

"Good morning to you too, Rosa," he says as he walks toward me. He presses a kiss to the top of my head and smiles when he sees my almost empty plate. "What's this?" he asks, picking up my application.

"My application for Café Au Lait. I need your address, though. I don't know it, and would it be okay if I used your phone number? I've never had a phone."

He looks at me, bewildered. "I'll give you a P.O. Box for your address. I don't want anyone knowing you live here, and I'll get you a phone. You'll have a phone number."

More to pay him back for? "I don't need a phone."

"Emilia, you need a phone," he insists in a firm tone. "I'll handle it."

I let out a loud sigh.

"Don't sigh at me. I want to do this." He smiles at me as he leans against the counter. "What's for breakfast, Rosa?"

Rosa sets down a plate in front of him just like she did for me, only with twice as much food. "Ah, *gracias*, Rosa. *Gracias.*"

She rolls her eyes at his charm and disappears down the hallway. Alex eats and I nervously strum my fingers on the granite counter.

"So, we should probably talk about last night," I say quietly, resting my chin in the palm of my hand.

"What about last night?" Alex asks casually, taking a spoonful of oatmeal.

I swallow, wondering what he'll think. "We probably shouldn't do that again."

"Why?" *Because I'm falling for you and when you get sick of me, which you will, I don't know if I'll be strong enough to just walk away from you.*

"I just don't want things to be weird with us. You know... roommates and all." I try to downplay my feelings for him by throwing out the "roommates" bit.

My eyes fall to the bowl in front of me and I take another bite of oatmeal. Alex sets his spoon on the plate and pushes it aside. "Last night was just the beginning, Emilia. I gave you the option to tell me no and you didn't. It'll happen again. Mark my words."

The beginning? Of what? He can't possibly want a relationship with me after one night. We barely know each other. Stammering, my cheeks heat with nerves and embarrassment. "But maybe this is a bad idea."

"Do you think this is a bad idea, Emilia?" He raises his eyebrows, looking through me instead of at me.

"I don't know," I admit weakly.

He softens at that, rubbing his hands up my forearms. "Then let what's supposed to happen, happen. Don't question everything."

His cell phone rings on the counter, and he reaches for it. Without another word, he answers and disappears down the hall and into his office. I lay my head on my arms and try to calm my racing heart. *"Let what's supposed to happen, happen."* If he had any idea what those words mean to me, he'd take them back.

I retreat back to my bathroom, where I apply some makeup and fluff my almost dry hair. Looking in the mirror, I take a deep breath and mentally give myself a pep talk before bringing my application to Café Au Lait. I need this job, and I can't let my nerves get the best of me. I need to push Alex out of my mind so I can focus and not sound like a fumbling idiot.

Slipping my feet into a pair of wedge sandals, I grab my wallet and head back to kitchen. I find my paper application on the counter where I left it, but there's a new cell phone on top of it. The address and phone number sections of my application have already been filled out. I smile as I pick up the phone and run my finger across the sleek touchscreen, bringing the phone to life. I cannot believe Alex would do this for me. He's too generous, but I appreciate that he's concerned about me. There are two contacts listed in the phone, Alex and Saul. I roll my eyes when I see Saul's name.

With my application in hand, I take the elevators down through the lobby. The old man from last night is sitting at the concierge desk, and his eyes widen in surprise as I approach.

"I'm Emilia. I think we got off to a rocky start." I extend my hand to him, and he takes it.

"I'm Fred. And yes, I would agree with you." He gives me a toothy grin. "Now that we've established you're with Mr. Estrada…" He pauses.

"Wait." I start to frown. "I'm not *with* Mr. Estrada. I'm not planning to stay here very long."

"They never do," I hear him mutter under his breath just as the elevator pings behind us.

What does that mean? Glancing over my shoulder, I catch Saul stepping out of the elevators, and I turn my attention back to Fred.

"I'm sorry, what were you saying?"

"Oh, nothing. Just be careful." His smile is tight now as he glances behind me to Saul.

"Nice to formally meet you, Fred."

"Nice to meet you too, Emilia. You let me know if you need *anything.*" He raises his eyebrows and tilts his head ever so slightly toward Saul. Fred must dislike Saul as much as I do.

"I will." I move quickly through the lobby and out onto the hot sidewalk in hopes of keeping Saul as far away as possible. He knows where I'm headed, but I have no intention of keeping him close. A shiver runs up my spine when I think of him following me all the time. I rush across the two blocks of bustling downtown Phoenix, back to Café Au Lait. Pushing the doors open, I inhale sharply the heavy scent of coffee infiltrating the shop.

The place is insanely busy. Every table is taken; even the couches are full. I notice Jax, the guy from yesterday, behind the counter, along with a pretty, middle-aged woman in an apron.

Jax nods at me when he sees me, and motions for me to step up. "Emilia, right?"

I nod and smile. "It's really busy. Now's probably not a good time to drop this off, huh?"

"Good as any. It's like this all the time." He smiles at me. His brown curly hair is pulled back into a ponytail or small bun, and his jawline is sprinkled with day-old stubble. His eyes crinkle ever so slightly at the corners when he smiles, and his bright blue eyes dance under his dark lashes. "Meg," he hollers. "This is Emilia."

He juts his head in my direction.

The woman behind the counter looks up from the coffee she's making and smiles. "Give me just a minute," she says as she pipes some whipped cream onto an order of steaming coffee.

I step back from the counter and right onto the feet of someone behind me. "I'm so sorry," I gasp as I spin around. My eyes instantly meet a pair of chocolate brown eyes attached to the body of a strikingly handsome man. A small smile tugs at the corner of his mouth as I apologize again. He's standing with another man and both are dressed professionally, wearing dark suits and ties.

Both men smile politely at my clumsiness. "Don't worry about it. There's not much room to move around in here," he says. His dark brown eyes are sincere, and I appreciate his kindness.

"There's not. It's so busy," I remark.

"Well, it's the best coffee downtown," he says conspiratorially, leaning in.

"Is it?"

"It is. Totally worth the wait." He smiles at me and extends his hand to me. "I'm Sam. Sam Cortez, and this is Trey Hoffman." His hand grips mine firmly before releasing it, and then I shake Trey's hand.

"Emilia Adams. Nice to meet both of you."

Trey pulls a ringing cellphone from his suit jacket and excuses himself, stepping outside.

"Can I buy you a coffee?" Sam's question catches me off guard.

"Oh, I'm just waiting to talk to the owner." I nod toward the woman behind the counter.

"So, let me buy you a coffee while you're waiting." His dark brown eyes sparkle against his tan skin.

"You don't have to do that," I respond nervously, my fingers scratching at my collarbone. Would it be weird to let a man buy me a coffee when I just left another man's bed? And what does that mean now that Alex and I have slept together? Should I not talk to other men? I shove those thoughts aside and smile politely at Sam.

"I know I don't have to. I'd like to," he says, stepping up to the counter. "I'll have a medium dark roast and she'll have..." He looks at me, waiting for my order.

"Same," I answer shyly. First Alex and now this? If I'd known what a friendly place Phoenix was going to be, I might have considered looking for my father years ago.

"She'll have the same," he repeats, and I smile at Jax, who takes our order. "Go grab that table, and I'll wait for the coffee," Sam instructs as he pulls out his wallet to pay just as a group leaves, opening up a table. I weave through the crowded shop and wait for Sam.

"Here you go." Sam hands me a cardboard cup with steaming coffee. It smells divine. Best coffee indeed.

"Thank you." I pull the plastic cap off the cup to let some of the steam out.

Sam pulls out the chair directly across from me and sits down. He glances at my application in the middle of the table but doesn't ask me about it. "Are you a student?" he asks, tearing open a packet of sugar.

"No. Not right now, anyway. Eventually, but I'm just looking for a job right now." I drum my fingers across the application before blowing into my cup, hoping it's cooled enough for me to sip. I can't wait to be a student again someday soon. I feel like I've missed out on the college experience, always having to work and take care of my mom.

Sam nods, satisfied with my answer. "How old are you, Emilia?" He smiles when he says my name.

"Twenty-one, why?" I barely refrain from frowning. I don't mind offering my age, but why would he care?

"Just curious." He shrugs, nonchalant.

My heart thrums nervously as we sit quietly sipping on our coffee, the air growing thick with silence. "So, do you and Trey work together?"

"We do. We share an office and an addiction to Café Au Lait's famous coffee." He grins.

"Are you from Phoenix? I mean, originally?" I ask him.

"Born and raised," he says with boyish pride. "What about you?"

"Just moved here from Illinois. Got tired of the cold," I lie to him. I'm tired of explaining my pathetic life. And he's a stranger. He doesn't need to know.

"You moved to the right place to escape the cold. I think it's supposed to be a hundred and fifteen today."

"I like the heat," I say, taking a sip of my coffee.

"Give it a year or two. You'll change your mind." He laughs.

Trey slips back inside and spots us. "Sorry to interrupt. I'm gonna grab a coffee to go, but we've gotta get back to the office." He gives Sam a concerned look and offers me a tight smile.

"It was nice to meet you, Emilia. Good luck with your interview."

"Thank you, and thanks for the coffee." I lift my cup in a salute. "I'm sorry again for stepping on you."

He winks, his eyes sparkling with amusement. "No apologies necessary."

Then Sam and Trey disappear down the street, walking quickly, just as Megan slides into the chair Sam was just in.

"Sorry to keep you waiting. Thank you for being so patient. As you can see, we're terribly understaffed." She sighs.

Megan and I instantly hit it off. We fall into easy conversation. She's convinced she can have me making coffee and serving pastries in no time. Thirty minutes later, I'm on my way back to Alex's condo, now a proud employee of Café Au Lait.

Fred is occupied on the phone as I move quietly through the lobby, and surprisingly, I don't see Saul. I exhale deeply, feeling a weight lifted off my shoulder. Money should start coming in soon, and I don't have Saul breathing down my neck. Letting myself into the condo, I'm surprised to find it empty. Alex isn't in his office, and Rosa is nowhere to be found. I find my way back to Alex's office and turn on his computer monitor. I open the internet browser and log into my email address, sending off a quick message to Carter to let him know that I've made it to Phoenix and found a job. I even give him my new cell phone number, just in case. As I'm about to hit send, a hand slaps the glass desk, startling me.

"What the fuck are you doing in here?" It's Saul, and he's seething.

I point at the screen to show him my email, but fear ripples through me, and I'm unable to form a coherent response. "Um, uh, I... uh..."

"Answer me," he snarls.

"I was sending an email to a family friend. That's all."

"Get out of this office."

My heart races a million miles an hour as I swivel in the chair and quickly hit send. I try to rush out, but Saul steps in front of me.

"If I ever catch you in this office again, you'll be sorry."

"Understood," I mumble as I step around him.

"Be careful, Emilia," I hear him say from the room as I leave. "What you know can get you killed around here." *What can get me killed?* I panic as I race toward the room I'm staying in. Every bone in my body is telling me to stay as far away from Saul as possible.

chapter seven

Alex

I SWERVE MY Range Rover to the side of the quiet neighborhood street and park under a tree. My car stands out in a neighborhood like this. Every house on this street is essentially the same cookie cutter design, all stucco with red tile roofs and painted tan. I pull my Glock from the center console and tuck it into the back waistband of my slacks, out of sight. I scan the street in front of me and behind me through the rearview mirror before quickly exiting my vehicle and striding down the street to one of my stash houses.

This house is being used to hold close to a million dollars' worth of marijuana. I rarely make an appearance at the houses. This is usually left up to my father and his crew, but alas, here I am. Fuck. I wipe a bead of sweat that is trickling down my temple. Pulling the phone from my pocket, I press the number for one of the guard's burners to alert him of my arrival.

I knock quietly, and Salvatore answers. "*Hola.*" He flicks the lock on the steel security door, and I step inside. The putrid smell of the bundled marijuana instantly hits my senses and I inwardly cringe. Some like the smell—me, I hate it.

"Kush?" I ask as I circle bundle after bundle of premium marijuana. I know the answer to this, but I need to verify. We import only the best—always have. Which makes our product highly sought after, compared to our competitors' shit.

"*Si.*" Salvatore nods, the scar on his forehead deepening with his scowl.

I set my hands on my hips. "I don't like all of this in one location. Have Roberto move half to the house on Sunset tonight."

"Yes, sir." He hesitates, then adds, "And, while you're here, I wanted to let you know we have a little problem with one of our guys…"

"Who?" I bark at Salvatore. My patience in dealing with personnel issues is wearing thin.

"Manuel."

"What about him?"

"He's, ahh… dipping into the goods at the house on Wheeler."

"Shit." I rake my hands over my face. Of all the fucking days. "Do we have anyone we can replace him with?" My mind races to count the men I have that aren't incarcerated.

"No. Everyone's still locked up."

"Shit. Okay, I'll handle Manuel. Get half of this moved tonight. Any other updates? Nosy neighbors? Anything else I need to be aware of?" I'm ready to get the fuck out of here. My Glock is digging a hole in my back.

"Nah, everything's been quiet. So far, so good." Sal shoves his hands into his front pockets.

"Good. We don't have any room for fuck-ups, Sal. I mean it."

He nods respectfully. "Yes, sir."

I clap my hand onto Salvatore's shoulder as a goodbye gesture. At the door, I peek through the peephole to make sure no one is outside before I slip back into the arid night. Two little girls ride past me on their bikes and smile, and I feel a hint of guilt knowing that I've brought my shit to their neighborhood, a neighborhood where they should feel safe, but at any minute could erupt into a goddamn warzone with one of our competitors or the feds. I swallow back my self-anger for bringing this into their world.

I slip out of the neighborhood and onto the freeway, heading over to the drop house on the west side. I hate these houses. I hate what we do in these houses. From the age of twelve, my dad was grooming me to run his business. He showed me everything—taught me that drugs, guns, and smuggling people into the States was the way to fast money. I despise this business. Gripping the steering wheel, I crawl along the freeway in rush-hour traffic, distracted by an incoming text from Emilia. As traffic stops, I glance at my phone.

I got the job!

I can actually see her excitement in the message and envision her giant smile. That sweet fucking smile I could stare at all day long. I respond quickly before tossing my phone into the cup holder.

Congrats. Celebrate tonight? Dinner?

I don't wait for her to respond. I'm not giving her a choice.

A few minutes later, I pull into an older neighborhood with rundown houses; a more appropriate place for the shit we do.

Cars are parked on the streets, in driveways, and all over front lawns. This neighborhood already looks like a war zone because it is. It's also easy to keep a drop house in a neighborhood like this because no one gives a shit about who's coming and going.

I dial Manuel's phone and tell him to expect me in a matter of minutes, then, just as my dad taught me, I park down the street and keep my head down as I approach the house. Loud music blares from a house two doors down, and sheets and blankets are makeshift curtains for the house next door. While my house is old, I make sure to keep it looking decent with ample window coverings and a manicured landscape. The less attention I draw to these houses the better, another lesson from my dad.

I knock twice and the door flies open. Manuel inhales sharply on a cigarette and steps aside to let me through.

"Boss," he exhales along with a puff of smoke.

I scowl at him. "Put that out. No smoking in the house."

He flicks the cigarette out the front door, then closes it behind him.

"How many are here?"

"Thirty, maybe forty."

"Jesus Christ, Manuel. I said no more than twenty per house."

"Eh, we picked up some extras. The extra cash is nice." He laughs and shrugs.

I grab him by the collar and slam him against the wall, speaking in a scarily quiet voice. "The more we have, the more likely we're going to get noticed. Move some," I bark at him.

His eyes flash with fear. "The other houses are full, boss."

"Get rid of them," I order. "Drop them off at the bus station or a park; just get rid of them. I want no more than twenty. Do you understand?" I let go of his shirt and step away.

He smells of sweat and cigarettes, and everything about him disgusts me. I hate dealing with these assholes.

"Yes, sir." Manuel takes a deep calming breath.

"And women. How many are women?" I told the men not to smuggle women. There's too much risk and liability. I don't want women or children harmed as we transport them across the country.

"Three, maybe." Manuel shoves his hands into the front pockets of his jeans.

My eyes narrow on him. "And how many have you been fucking?"

He stands quietly. *God-fucking-dammit.*

"You've been told before." I have to clench my fists to keep from caving in his face. "You do not touch the women. Why is that so hard for you?"

"Hey, they're willing. It's not like I'm forcing myself on 'em."

I lower my voice. "Don't. Touch. The women. *Comprende?*"

He nods frantically. "Yes, sir."

"And clean this place up. It's a fucking mess." I can hear pots and pans being shuffled in the kitchen, and I glance at Manuel.

"Pablo," he promises. "He's getting food ready."

I back slightly away, but keep my eyes narrowed. "You make sure they're well cared for. No one goes hungry or gets hurt in one of my houses."

"Your father was never this demanding," Manuel mutters sulkily.

I grit my teeth. Well, if my father were here, then I wouldn't have to be. "I'm not my father. I'm running this show right now.

You answer to me. If you have a problem with that, let me know. I'll take care of it right now." I reach into my waistband and pull the gun out.

Manuel's eyes get big and he holds up both hands in defeat. "No problem, Alejandro. No problem."

"Good." I put the Glock back in its place. "I'll be back tomorrow. I want this place cleaned up. No more than twenty and no women. Understood?"

"*Si.*"

Back in my car, I lock the doors and rest my head back, closing my eyes for just a moment... until I remember that I'm a fucking target sitting here in the dark with my eyes closed. I hate every single part of this business—I hate being a criminal. Pushing the ignition button on my car, I throw the gear in drive and speed out of this shitty neighborhood.

THE DOOR SLAMS unusually hard behind me, and I find Rosa in the kitchen, chopping fruit and humming to herself.

"*Mijo,*" she says when she looks up and sees me. "What's wrong?"

"Just a really long day." I rub my temples and realize how exhausted I am.

She slices strawberries at expert speed and tosses them into a ceramic bowl. "Emilia told me you were celebrating tonight, so I didn't make dinner. I just wanted you to have something for breakfast. I'll be late tomorrow morning. I'm stopping at the grocery store on my way over. Is there anything you need me to pick up?"

What would I do without Rosa? "Not that I can think of. If I think of anything, I'll call you. Thanks, Rosa."

"Have fun tonight. Oh, and *mijo*." She leans in conspiratorially. "I really like Emilia. We got to spend some time together today. She's a good girl."

That makes me smile. The first one since I walked in the door. "I know. I like her too. A lot."

Rosa sets the knife on the cutting board and looks at me seriously. "Be good to her."

I nod. "I intend to."

I find Emilia asleep, curled up in the fetal position on her bed with a pillow pressed to her stomach. Her long hair is splayed on the pillow beneath her, her shoulders rising and falling ever so slightly with each quiet breath. She looks so peaceful when she sleeps. I lean over her and press a light kiss to her forehead.

She hums and rolls slowly to her back. "You're home," she says without opening her eyes.

"How did you know it was me?"

She rubs her eyes and smiles. "Your cologne. I love the smell of it."

I take a seat on the edge of the bed. "Think about what you want for dinner. I have to shower, then we can head out."

"What do you want?" she asks. Of course she wouldn't think of herself. If I've learned anything about her these last few days, it's that she's the most unselfish creature I've ever known.

Her fingers trace circles on my forearm, and I get goose bumps from her touch. "You. That's all I want." I wink at her. The stress from earlier washes away with each circle her soft finger traces on my arm. Being around her breathes life into me.

She laughs, placing her hand across her belly. Her laugh is contagious. "You can have me for dessert. But what do you want for dinner?"

"This is your dinner," I tell her, combing through her hair, which is still splayed behind her. "You get to choose."

She frowns. "Honestly, I don't know. We never really ate out."

And there it is again, that guilt. I have everything and more, and she's gotten by with next to nothing. "How about steak? I know a great steakhouse."

She smiles the most sincere smile at me. "Then dessert back here, okay?"

I couldn't agree more. "Deal."

AT A SMALL table in a dimly lit corner of the steakhouse, a candle flickers in the center of the linen-clad table, and Emilia rubs her arms with her hands.

"It's cold in here," she says with a shiver.

I pull off my sport coat and hand it to her, but she holds up a hand. "You don't have to do that."

"I want to. You're cold. I want you to enjoy dinner, not freeze to death."

She smiles and slides the jacket over her shoulders. "Why are you always so nice to me?"

Should I not be? I don't know why, but that statement makes me sad, but I simply tell her, "You make it easy."

The waiter interrupts us and takes our drink and dinner

orders. So far, the conversation has been minimal, the evening quiet. Emilia runs her finger around the rim of her water glass, her gaze far away.

"Penny for your thoughts." I reach out and rest my hand on hers.

She looks up from her water glass and sadness flashes through her eyes. "My mom used to say that."

"I'm sorry, I didn't mean to bring up any bad memories."

"You didn't." She smiles softly. "Even though she was horribly depressed, she could always read me. She knew when I had something on my mind and always tried her best to listen."

"What's bothering you?" I give her hand a gentle squeeze. I want her to trust me—talk to me.

It takes her a moment, but finally, she sighs. "Alex, something happened today—with Saul."

My body immediately goes rigid. "What? Tell me." I've always trusted Saul because my father has—but the look of fear in Em's eyes has me second-guessing Saul's intentions.

"I was in your office." She hesitates, looking upset. "I sat down at your desk…"

My heart begins racing as I mentally scroll through what I might have left on the desk. I'm always meticulous and discreet with messages and information, but I've been so exhausted lately, so I fear I've become sloppy. "What did you see?" I ask as calmly as possible, keeping my face neutral.

"Huh?" She blinks at me. "Nothing. I was checking my email. That's all. But Saul came in and yelled at me. He told me that knowing too much will get me killed." Her hand started shaking and she pulled it into her lap.

I inhale sharply. *Motherfucker.* "I'll talk to him."

"I promise I wasn't doing anything other than sending an email. I assumed you'd rather me use your computer than go to the library."

"You're fine, Emilia." I'm not entirely comfortable with her in my office, but she didn't do anything wrong.

"What did he mean, though?" she asks, curious and wary at the same time.

I cringe internally. Saul has always been loyal to my father, to his business, but he's had a chip on his shoulder ever since I started changing things.

"Nothing." I force a smile. "Saul is dramatic. He understands my business, and he's just looking out for me. I apologize for him. *No one* will ever hurt you." And yet another lie falls from my tongue. Because, while I can promise that I won't hurt her directly, I can't promise that no one else will. That I'm not putting her in danger as we speak.

Setting those thoughts aside, I bump my foot against hers again under the table and find her gaze.

The waiter arrives and pours a small sample of wine. I approve and he pours two glasses before disappearing. In an effort to change the subject, I raise my glass to toast Emilia's new job.

"Congratulations, Em." I love calling her that; it makes me feel like she'll be more permanent in my life, which both terrifies and excites me. "May this be the first of many celebrations."

Her smile is sweet and soft. "Thank you."

"I'M STUFFED." EMILIA rubs her stomach and exhales loudly. "This place was amazing."

"It's one of my favorite restaurants. I don't come here that often."

"Well, thank you for bringing me here—but I hope you saved room for dessert." Her voice is suggestive, but she giggles, and a blush crawls across her cheeks.

"What's on the menu?"

"A little of this, a little of that." She smirks. Fuck, she's adorable.

I open my wallet and throw five hundred dollars cash on the table. It's more than enough to cover our bill twice over, but I don't care. I stand up and reach for Emilia's hand. "Let's go." Her eyes bulge at the wad of cash on the table. "Let's go, Emilia." It's an order.

The car ride home is quiet. My cock throbs inside my pants in anticipation of all the things I want to do to Emilia for "dessert." She keeps her attention out the window, taking in the sights of downtown Phoenix as we weave through the streets back to my condo. I reach across the console and rest my hand on her knees. She bobs it slowly as we head toward home.

In the garage, I see Andres waiting near the elevators. "There's someone I want you to meet." I squeeze our joined hands.

She sees Andres and her eyes widen in concern. I can understand why. Andres is huge; six-foot-three and easily two seventy-five of solid muscle. There's no one else I'd trust more to protect Emilia.

"Em, this is Andres. Andres, this is Emilia."

"Nice to meet you, ma'am," he says quietly, reaching out to

shake her hand. She doesn't reciprocate. Instead, she stares down at her feet. I clear my throat and nod at Andres. I filled him in this morning on the phone about Emilia's concerns and her hesitancy at having someone with her.

"Emilia, Andres is going to be your security. I promise you won't even know he's there. It's more for my peace of mind than anything."

"Then I don't need him," she interjects, pulling away from me. "This is about you. Not me. I'm not your girlfriend or your business partner. I know nothing about your business. I'm your roommate. This charade is silly." She steps around Andres, pushing the button to call the elevator.

I flex my hands and grind my teeth. Her roommate; that's all I am, according to her. Regardless, she's not going out there without protection. "I thought we were past this, Emilia. It's not open for negotiation."

She sighs loudly and turns to face Andres and me. "I work at a coffee shop. I'm a twenty-one-year-old girl who's flown under the radar my entire life. I don't need protection." The doors slide open, and she steps inside. "I'll see you upstairs." She leans against the back wall, and I watch her intently as the doors close, leaving Andres and me alone.

"She's a stubborn one." Andres smirks.

"She'll come around. Until then, stay back. Keep her in view, but give her space," I inform him, rubbing my forehead.

"Are we expecting anything, or is this strictly precaution?"

"Precaution only. There's been some intel, though, that Mendes is looking to make a move. We're weak right now. Half our guys are locked up or... well, you know the story, and I'm working with a skeleton crew. They're looking to disable us even

further, and I just worry she's going to get caught in the middle."
My worst fucking nightmare. Whatever Emilia and I are to each other,
she's innocent. I couldn't bear it if she got hurt. "Plus the ATF
and Agent Cortez are watching me like a fucking hawk."

Andres nods in understanding. "Personal question, and you
don't have to answer," Andres says. "You've never kept a woman
around before. Why now?"

I don't know how to answer, or if I should. I just know I
need Emilia as much as she needs me. I feel peace in her
presence, a sense of good within me. "We're done here.
Goodnight, Andres."

He nods curtly. "Night, boss."

I find Emilia sitting on the floor outside the condo. "What're
you doing?"

"I don't have a key."

I'll have to remedy that. I reach out and pull her up. "I've got
a spare inside."

"Alex," she says quietly from behind me. I've opened the
door and am standing just inside the condo while she remains in
the foyer just outside. "You're going to have to trust me, you
know."

We both stand there silently for a moment. I'm not sure
what to think of that. I've never been wholly trusting of anyone
other than my mother—but everything inside me tells me Emilia
might be the one to break down those walls and let me trust
again.

She steps over the threshold and stops in front of me. "In a
matter of days, I've moved into your house, I've slept in your bed,
and now you're paying someone to watch me. You're going to
have to trust me enough to tell me why I'm important enough to

keep alive—because I'm not important."

Does she really believe that? "You're important to me, Emilia."

"I've never been important to anyone before," she mumbles as she leans into me and wraps her arms around my neck, burying her face in my chest. I wrap my own arms around her, and we embrace each other. The action is simple and yet complex. I feel so much just holding her, and for a few moments, everything in my world feels right.

"I have a surprise for you," she says as she pulls away from me, moving toward the kitchen.

"I don't like surprises," I tease her. Pressing the switch on the wall, the kitchen comes to life under the bright lights.

"You'll like this, I promise." Her smile is big, and her eyes exude a certain happiness I'm not sure I've seen in her yet. She looks peaceful, content. She opens the refrigerator and pulls out a large metal mixing bowl.

"Here." She sets the bowl on the island and pulls out two large metal spoons from a drawer. Inside the bowl is a ball of chocolate chip cookie dough. "I made it for you. We don't have to bake it if you don't want to." She smiles at me again. "But if you get salmonella, don't blame it on me." She laughs. I'm speechless and my throat tightens when I think about how my mom and I would stand around our small kitchen, digging spoons into the raw cookie dough. For Emilia to remember what I told her about my mom touches me.

She hands me a metal spoon, and I scoop out a large spoonful of the dough and put it in my mouth.

"Does it taste okay?" She cringes, waiting for my reaction.

"It's delicious." Not a lie, for once. "You didn't have to do this, though. Rosa could've made it."

She shrugs, blushing. "I wanted to. That's why I was in your pantry the other night."

Ah, so that was why. "I wondered what you were doing naked in my pantry." The image of that night makes my cock throb again, reminding me that we're back home, in my condo.

"I wasn't naked," she says teasingly.

"Close enough." I take another spoonful and, this time, feed it to Emilia. Her pink lips wrap around the spoon as she pulls the dough off and into her mouth.

"Mmm," she hums as she savors it, causing my cock to twitch again. Just being around her arouses me, but the little noises she makes completely turn me on. I set the spoon on the counter and pull her into me, pressing my lips to hers.

"This dessert was amazing, but I'm greedy. I want more than just cookie dough," I say to her in between kisses.

She smiles against my lips. "Oh yeah? What else did you have in mind?"

I lace her fingers through mine and walk her to my bedroom, stopping at the edge of the bed. We stand and take each other in, unspoken desires bubbling at the surface. She stands timidly, her eyes darkening with need before she turns around and pulls her hair over her shoulder so I can unzip her dress. My fingers caress the base of her neck as I slowly pull down on the metal zipper, releasing the fabric. I watch the black dress fall to the floor in a pile around her feet. She kicks off her shoes, then waits for me to make the next move.

God, she's beautiful. Everything about her is pure—good, and for every moment I'm with her, I want to be a better man, a man she deserves. But under the desire to do good, lives a monster. I shake those thoughts from my head and unclasp her black bra. She stands with her back to me in nothing more than a pair of panties. I trail my fingers down her spine, and for the first time, really feel how frail she is. "Turn around," I whisper, and she does. Her arms drop from her waist and settle at her sides while I take in the sight of her from head to toe.

"May I?" she asks, tilting her head as she reaches for the buttons on my dress shirt.

I nod in approval, and her long fingers press the buttons through each hole. She takes her time running her hands over each arm and down my stomach. Tugging on the undershirt, she tugs it free from my pants and pushes it up and over my head before moving to unfasten my leather belt. The belt is the next item on the floor, then my pants. Before she's able to go any further, I stop her with one hand to her neck.

I squeeze her neck gently. "I can't promise you more than this, Emilia." It's just sex. I can't give her more, and she deserves more than the broken dreams, lies, and deceit that I can offer her. My world will hurt her, maybe even destroy her. She is good and I am evil.

Her eyes soften, and she nods.

I pinch one of her nipples and elicit a loud gasp. She steps into me. Her fingers tremble as she runs them over my chest, coming to a rest at the waistband of my boxer briefs. I guide her to the bed, stopping her just long enough to remove her panties before coaxing her to lie down.

She watches intently as I remove my remaining clothes and lie down next to her. "The lights," she says shyly, her arm draped over her stomach.

I shake my head. "I want to see all of you, feel all of you." I position myself on top of her and watch her shift from timid to hungry as I pull one of her breasts into my mouth. "I'm going to taste every inch of you." I pull her other breast into my mouth, circling the stiff nipple. "I'm going to explore all of you, leaving nothing untouched." I reach between her legs and slide my fingers over her clit.

She gasps.

"You like that, don't you?" I brush over her again, this time slipping a finger inside her. She's wet... and warm... and I have no self-control when it comes to her. I push her knees apart and taste her. She's sweet and salty and perfection. She gasps and lifts her hips from the bed when my tongue circles around her sweet clit. "I need to be inside you," I hiss as I pull back and then slip inside her. A primal growl escapes me as I settle into her. Her fingers scratch my back, and she moans.

"Jesus, Em." I still, allowing her to adjust to me, but she lifts her hips and guides me to move.

"You feel so good," she whispers as her nails scratch a gentle path down my back. Her long legs are wrapped around my hips, her feet pressed against my ass. She moans with each thrust, eyes glazed and skin flushed.

I slow my pace, finally stopping. Her breaths are shallow and quick as I pull out and guide her to roll over. "On your knees, chest to the bed." I want her ass in the air. I need to feel her from behind.

I ease myself into her again, and she moans loudly. I'm deeper, and with each thrust, I can feel her walls begin to constrict. My fingers dig into the contours of her tight ass, my release building. Leaning forward, I reach around and squeeze her neck, gently pulling her back into me, harder. A few more thrusts, and I spill my release into her. Releasing her neck, I reach down and slide her throbbing clit between my fingers, bringing her to climax.

After, we lie next to each other, catching our breaths. She places her hand on my chest, a gesture of connectedness on some deeper level. It's just the right amount of closeness for whoever we are to each other.

We lie in comfortable silence until I feel her hand fall from my chest and the bed shift as she moves to the edge.

"Where're you going?" I ask, startling her.

"To my room." She reaches down to pick up her dress and lingerie from the floor.

"No. You're sleeping with me." As much as I don't want her getting attached to me, I need her here in bed with me.

"Alex," she says. "I should go to my room."

"Lie down with me. Please." I pull the covers back on the bed, and she stands hesitantly, glancing between me and the door before dropping her clothes to the floor and sliding back into my bed. She puts distance between us, but I won't allow it. Reaching over, I pull her to me. Skin to skin, we lie vulnerable next to each other. We've shared the most intimate of acts, and I feel connected to her on a level I've never experienced, yet I can't bring myself to let her in. I can't let who I am destroy her, and if she gets too close, I will.

My fingers run a trail from the hollow of her neck, my favorite place on her body, down her chest, through her breasts, and back again. It's comforting to feel her pressed against me, the light floral scent of her shampoo filling the pillow we share.

"Tell me about your mom," she whispers, her voice breaking the silence.

"What do you want to know?" I should've evaded mentioning my mother. I never talk about my mom. It's personal. Too painful.

"Everything. What she was like. What you loved about her."

I swallow hard, but feel words coming to me. I shouldn't tell her and yet I do. "I loved everything about her. She was always calm, caring. She gave everything to make others happy." I choke back the lump I feel forming in my throat. "She loved to cook and bake—her life was her family."

"How old were you when she passed?" She draws small circles on my chest with her finger. Her touch is comforting— calming.

"Six, almost seven. It was a week before my seventh birthday. I never celebrated a birthday after that. She was what made birthdays special for me. She made everything special. Every holiday, every meal, every bedtime story. We'd pray and read stories every night. We were inseparable. My dad's business was just taking off, and he wasn't around a lot, but my mom made up for that. She'd walk us to school every morning and meet us in the courtyard every afternoon. On our walks home, we'd talk about our day, and she'd tell us what she'd made for dinner. I'll never forget the day she wasn't there to meet us. You know how they say your gut knows when something is wrong?"

"Mm-hmm."

I exhale a heavy breath. "I just knew it was bad when she wasn't there. I ran home as fast as I could. We lived about a half-mile from the school, but I was in a full sprint. My brother was behind me, I'm not sure how far behind because I never looked back. I ran and ran until I got home. The front door was open. I didn't hesitate. Nothing mattered other than knowing where my mother was. I screamed for her, Em. I screamed so loud, and she never answered. I searched the kitchen, her bedroom, my bedroom. I'll never forget how hard my heart was pounding." I pause to collect my thoughts, my emotions.

Emilia pulls herself even closer to me, pressing her cheek to my chest, and draping her arm across me. She weaves her long, bare legs in between mine, holding onto me like a vise grip. What I'd normally consider smothering is actually comforting. Her softness draped over me is comforting like nothing I've ever experienced.

"I finally checked her bathroom," I continue, only barely aware that I'm combing my fingers through her hair. "The bathroom door was closed, but she loved baths. I thought maybe she'd lost track of time and was in the bathtub. I knocked, she didn't answer, and that's when I opened the door." My voice cracks. "She was lying on the floor, covered in blood. She'd been shot three or four times. There were two holes in her head. I'll never forget her face. I'll never get that image out of my mind." I squeeze my arms around her.

"I'm so sorry, Alex," Emilia whispers. "I know exactly what you're feeling."

"You do?" I snap. How could she possibly?

"I do," she says sadly. "It was only ever my mom and me, and I also found her dead with a bullet hole to her head. If anyone understands what you're feeling, it's me."

Fuck. I lay silent. I want so badly to argue with her, but it's not worth it. She got the best years of her life with her mom… I didn't.

"I didn't mean to snap at you," I apologize. "I just don't talk about her—ever," I admit.

"I know I'm just a stranger to you, Alex… but you can always talk to me." She squeezes me tighter. I run my hand through her long hair again and press a kiss to her forehead.

There's so much I'd love to tell her—but I can't.

chapter eight

Emilia

I DON'T KNOW what time it is, but Alex has been restless ever since he told me about his mom. He's been tossing and turning, and when I try to come closer, he manages to push me away. Once again, he rolls to his back and flings both arms above his head, releasing a loud sigh. I hesitate before making my move. Rolling over, I push myself up and straddle him.

"You're agitated," I tell him. He brings his arms down to hold my hips, his fingertips digging into the soft flesh just above my hipbones. "I'm sorry if I made you angry."

"I'm not angry," he says, his voice void of emotion.

I gently rock my hips over his cock and feel it begin to harden beneath me. I want to help him release some of his tension, but he's resisting. He holds my hips firmly, not allowing me to move on top of him. Leaning forward, I press soft kisses to his chest. I make my way to his neck and nip at the soft skin just above his collarbone. My hands sink into the soft mattress on either side of his head, and he finally relents, dropping his hands from my hips. He moans when I lift myself to allow his cock to stand up. Gently guiding myself onto him, he slides in comfortably and fills me completely. I moan at the sensation of him filling me. Placing both hands on his chest, I guide myself up and down, my pussy clenching his long shaft with each movement. He finally succumbs, and I can feel him begin to relax beneath me. His eyes are dark with desire and he presses his fingers into the soft skin of my waistline.

I rise and fall, my movements quicker and unyielding, his fingertips squeezing me harder. "Need you," I mumble as my head falls back, his cock brushing against my G spot and taking my breath away.

"What did you say?" he asks as he lifts his hip and drives himself into me.

"I said I need you."

He stills and closes his eyes for a moment before slowly picking up his pace. The pressure of his pelvic bone against my clit sends me spiraling into an orgasm that has my body trembling. I lean forward on his chest while he slams into me once more with his release, then I lie on top of him, just feeling him—all of him. Silence fills the space between us again, and I can feel his conflict. He holds on to me like he can't let go, like he'll die without me. But the pain on his face tells another story, the real story—he can and will live without me. When he finally speaks, his words are strained. "Em, I can't—"

"I know," I say, cutting him off. I slide off of him and curl into a ball next to him. His hand rests on my side, and I hear the steady rhythm of his light breaths. A small part of me wants to run, retreat to the safety of the guest room, and guard my heart. But somewhere deep inside of me, another part of me longs for

Alex's love—even if this is all he can give. I will compromise and take what he can give me—even if this is all it ever is.

I WAKE UP in my own bed, the sunlight crawling across my face. I never closed the curtains last night. I roll over and yelp when I see Alex on the chaise lounge. He's wearing a pair of gym shorts and nothing else, and he offers me a tired smile.

"What're you doing in here?" I pull the sheet up higher over my naked body, even though we've seen each other naked several times already. I feel vulnerable with him right there, especially after last night.

"I like watching you sleep. You're peaceful." His voice is weak, tired, but he chuckles a little and points at me. "Nothing I haven't already seen."

I pull the sheet a little higher, hating the blush creeping across my cheeks. "How long have you been sitting there?"

"A few hours."

"You should really go get some sleep."

"I wanted to watch you sleep."

The whites of his eyes are bloodshot, and dark circles are starting to form underneath. His hair is a disheveled mess—but he still looks perfect to me. He scratches his chest lightly, rolling the crucifix in his fingers.

"Em, when you think about your future, what is it that you see? What do you want?" His face is full of anguish.

I frown and think about it. Last night, he got angry with me, and now he's asking me *this*? "That's a big question for..."

I look around for a clock.

"Five thirty in the morning," he answers. "Tell me."

I have to think for a moment. "I mean, I think we all have dreams. What we'd like or how we think our lives will turn out, but I also think that ninety-nine percent of the time those realities don't exist… at least not for me."

"Why do you say that?" he questions, lacing his fingers behind his head. His face is full of confusion and mixed emotions.

I shrug. "Just my life. I try not to be negative, but when I think things can't get worse, they usually do."

He seemed pained by my answer. "So, what do you envision for your future?"

I sigh softly. "I stopped thinking so far ahead a long time ago. I just try to live for today."

"Em, answer me." His eyes plead with me. "We all think about where we'll be in five or ten years."

Not me. Still, I do dream. I do want. I do. "Sure; I have the same dream every girl has—get married, have kids, live happily ever after. I want to be the mom that mine could never be for me." I shrug, although I feel the hurt wound tight inside of me. "What do you want?" I need to take the focus off me.

"I'd fucking love all of that," he says quietly, introspective, then he rubs his tired eyes and leans back against the chaise lounge.

"Then have it," I tell him. "If you want it bad enough—go get it."

He turns his head to look at me, but he's still lost in his thoughts. There are a million questions, a million concerns, running through those dark, tired eyes.

"It doesn't work that way," he says.

"Sure it does. If you want something badly enough, you'll make it happen."

His shoulders slump with defeat or exhaustion—I'm not sure which. "Come here."

He pats his lap, and I take the sheet with me, sitting there. Immediately, he snakes an arm around my waist and pulls me closer. Brushing the hair off my shoulders, he runs his fingers across my collarbone and rubs the front of my neck, resting his finger at the base in the hollow. If I had to guess, I would say this is his favorite spot on my body.

"Why are you so beautiful?" he whispers reverently.

"I'm not." I run my hand up the side of his cheek, feeling the soft hair that sits along his jawline. I cup his cheek, and his head falls into my palm. His eyes soften as my thumb brushes the soft skin just below his eye. "Why are you so handsome?"

He blows a puff of air through his nose and rolls his eyes at me.

"You are. You're handsome and kind… and—"

"Stop." He winces.

"No. This is what I see when I'm with you." He has to know how beautiful he is, how kind it was of him to take me in, even if I was terrified of him that first day.

"You don't know anything about me, Em. This"—He gestures up and down his body—"is smoke and mirrors. It's a mask for the evil I am inside."

I almost laugh. *Evil?* Why would he think that about himself? "You're not evil." I place my hand on his chest, over his heart.

"I am." Our eyes lock on each other, and behind those amber orbs I see a world of hurt—despair. His thumbs rub circles over my collarbone, and I lean forward, capturing his lips. His soft, warm lips. I press a light kiss, and he kisses me back. "Will you go somewhere with me?"

Anywhere, but I don't say that. "Sure. Where?"

"Church."

My eyes must widen until he smirks and runs a finger over my lip. "I go every Sunday, and sometimes a couple times during the week, and for sure on every holy day."

I nod slowly in surprise. "I've never been to church, but I'll go with you. I need to shower and get ready…"

"You have plenty of time. Mass isn't until nine. Rosa will have brunch waiting when we get back." He smiles warmly at me and his mood seems to have turned.

"Okay then. Church it is," I say with a breathy laugh.

THREE HOURS LATER, we're walking the quiet downtown Phoenix streets. A light breeze makes the air around us feel like an oven. We approach a giant stucco church that sits right in the heart of downtown. It's old, but beautiful and clearly renovated. Alex reaches for my hand as we take the steep steps to the heavy, oak double doors with large wrought-iron handles. Just inside, Alex dips his finger in a small cup of water secured to the wall and makes the sign of the cross. Then he dips his finger again and makes the sign of the cross on my forehead.

"Holy water," he says quietly.

He guides me into the church and we find a wooden pew in the back. Before sitting down, Alex pulls down a small, padded bench and kneels, bowing his head. I sit quietly and simply take in the beauty. Large pillars adorn the inside, and stained-glass windows cast a glow over the entire place. The altar is simple, yet elegant, a crucifix hanging prominently behind the altar. Such history here.

Alex remains kneeling in prayer for quite some time, and I observe people of all walks of life filter soundlessly into the church and take their seats. An organ plays a slow, haunting song, and the entire congregation suddenly rises. I stand and Alex slips his hand into mine again. For the next hour, I watch as everyone rises, sits, kneels, and Alex stays with me as everyone leaves to take communion, as he calls it. He's whispered to me throughout the mass, informing me of what's happening or what's about to happen.

I'm oddly at peace here. I talk to my mom and feel like maybe she can hear me, and I pray to God, hoping maybe he'll hear me too. My hopes are low, seeing as I've asked for so little in the past and every prayer has seemingly gone unanswered before.

Alex wraps his arm around my shoulders, pulling me to him, and I find myself sinking into his side. I rest my head on his shoulder and close my eyes as we listen to the priest give his final prayer. Alex's body is warm, and I can smell his cologne that I love so much. Between the comfort of his touch and the peacefulness of the place, I feel a sense of contentment pass through me.

"So, what did you think?" Alex asks me as we walk down the steps to the street below.

"It's weird." I turn to look at him. "I feel happier."

He smiles at me. "It does that to you. You leave your troubles, your burdens, in that church and when you walk away, you feel lighter."

"That's exactly it. I feel lighter."

"I want to introduce you to someone," he says, reaching for my hand. He pulls me through the sea of people that have gathered outside to socialize.

"Father Mark." He nods at the priest. "I wanted to introduce you to someone. This is Emilia. Emilia Adams."

"Ah, Emilia!" he says excitedly. "Alejandro has told me about you."

Confused, I look at Alex, then back to the priest. "He has?"

"He has." He smiles at me. Father Mark adjusts his wire-rimmed glasses and looks between Alex and me.

"Well, it's a pleasure to meet you," I tell him, shaking his hand. I'm shocked. Twice now, I've been told Alex has mentioned me.

"Likewise." He nods. "Alex, would you mind if I had a word with you?"

"Sure, Father." Alex gives me a reassuring smile. "We'll be just a minute."

"I'll just wait over here." I gesture to a tall tree full of blooming flowers, and Father Mark guides Alex through the crowd. The two men lean into each other and disappear from my sight. I wait in the shade of the tree and people watch. I find myself doing this a lot in Phoenix. At home, everyone looked the same, acted the same—here, it's eclectic, different.

"I thought that was you," I hear just as someone touches my arm, catching me off guard.

"Oh my gosh, Sam! You scared me." I laugh and cover my heart with my hands.

"I didn't expect to see you here. I've never seen you here

before," he says as he glances around, his dark brown eyes dancing in the sunrays that peek through the branches of the tree we're standing under.

"It's my first time here—actually my first time ever going to church." I'm somewhat embarrassed to admit that.

He furrows his brows like it's the craziest thing he's ever heard anyone say. "Ever?"

"Ever." I laugh.

"So, what did you think?" He rolls up the sleeves on his white dress shirt and loosens his purple and gray necktie.

"I liked it enough that I'll probably come back." I shrug, not wanting to share my true personal story of how it was. I certainly don't know him well enough for that.

"Good." He nods, as he nudges my shoulder. "I'm glad I got to see you. I'd ask you to join me for coffee or breakfast, but I have to work today."

I frown at him. "On a Sunday?"

"Yeah, we've got a lot going on. Some new shit just landed on my desk, and it's the kind of work that can't wait for Monday."

My eyes widen when Sam says "shit" right outside a church. "Well then, you better get to work. Corporate America awaits." He looks at me funny, but smiles and I add, "Anyway, I'm sure I'll see you at Café Au Lait sometime, right?"

"I was just going to ask you if you got the job. I take it you did?" He wiggles his eyebrows comically.

I nod, feeling proud, even though it's just a coffee shop. It's a step in the right direction, in a new town that I still don't know. It's a huge step for me. "I did."

"Congratulations." He grins. "When do you start?"

"Tomorrow." Megan asked me to start on Monday so she

could train someone else she also just hired this weekend. It's easier for her to manage training us one at a time.

"Great. Well, then, I'll see you tomorrow. Enjoy the rest of your day, Emilia."

"See you tomorrow." I watch Sam disappear through the now thinning crowd and smile at the little flutter in my stomach. Much like the feeling I get when I see Alex walking back toward me.

"Everything okay?" I ask him.

"Yeah. He just wanted to chat about some things." He offers me a reassuring smile, but his eyes search the people gathered around us. "Let's go. Rosa will have brunch waiting for us." He laces his fingers through mine and guides me back toward the condo.

"So, you're pretty close to Father Mark?"

"I am. He baptized me as a baby and has given me all my sacraments since." *Sacraments?* I'll ask him later what that means as I have a more pressing thing nagging me. "I was surprised when he said you had mentioned me."

He chuckles. "Yeah. Part of my penance is to do good for strangers. I mentioned that you had moved in."

"Ah, see… I'm just a stranger and a good deed." I nudge him with my shoulder, but my heart hurts at this reference.

"You were," he admits softly, something deeper in his tone. "You're more than that now, Em. Funny how that works."

I'm not sure what he means, but I'm afraid if I ask him to clarify that I won't like the answer, so I remain quiet and don't push the conversation any further. Along the way, he points out things of interest—an outdoor air mall, a salon, a small city park, and two college campuses; all tucked together within a few-block radius. I never realized how beautiful and clean downtown Phoenix was until just now.

The condo smells amazing when we return, and it's amazing how at home I feel here now. For the short time I've been here, this feels like home, as scared as that thought still makes me.

I can hear Rosa in the kitchen, humming, and the sounds of pots and pans moving about the stove. She's not quiet, but she knows how to cook better than anyone I've ever met.

"Good morning, Rosa!" Alex says loudly as we come into the kitchen.

Rosa looks up and smiles at Alex. "*Mijo, mija.* How was church? Did you pray for me?"

"I did, Rosa." He kisses her sweetly on the cheek.

She laughs and smacks his arm playfully. I love how they are with each other. It says a lot about a man, the way he is with his mother. And even though Alex's mother is gone, Rosa is somewhat a replacement, a surrogate, in a way.

"Brunch is ready. I'm going to take off." Rosa continues fluttering about. "Just leave the dishes in the sink, and I'll take care of them when I get back in a few hours."

"Thank you, Rosa. It looks amazing."

"You're welcome. *Eat!*" She pinches my hip and scoots around me. Pulling her purse off the counter, she disappears down the hall, and I hear the door close behind her.

Alex begins taking out plates and silverware. "Do you want to eat in the dining room, or in here?"

"Here." I pat the island. "No need to move everything to the other room."

There's a giant bowl of fresh cut fruit, scrambled eggs, bacon, and Belgian waffles.

"Rosa must really like you; she doesn't cook like this for me." He winks at me.

"Whatever." I chuckle. "She treats you like a spoiled little brat," I tease him as I plate up a waffle and fruit.

"She should. I pay her a small fortune."

"Have you always had someone cook and clean for you?" I ask, curious.

He thinks for a moment, scooping eggs onto his plate. "Not always. I mean, when my mom was alive, she did all of that. Then, after she died and my dad was building his business, we had someone. She was kind of a nanny, a housekeeper, and a cook all rolled into one. She basically raised me."

"What happened to her?"

"What do you mean?" He gives me side eyes.

"Where is she now?"

"Oh, she moved back to Mexico. Her mother lived there, and when I graduated from high school, she moved back to take care of her. I think my dad still talks to her now and then." He shrugs. "So, after I graduated from college and bought this place, I needed someone to help me stay on top of everything, and that's when I found Rosa."

"I really like her. She's spunky." She's full of energy and wit, and I find myself smiling every time I'm around her.

He laughed softly. "That's a word you don't hear every day, but yeah, she's pretty amazing."

"So, what did you get your degree in?" I ask as I smother my waffle in syrup. Undeniably the best part of this entire breakfast is the thick, sweet maple syrup.

"Business with a focus in accounting. I'm a numbers guy." He smirks. "What about you? Did you ever go to college?"

"I took a few classes at the local community college, but then took some time off to work more. We needed the money more than I needed to take classes." I long for the day I'll be able to go back to school and finish my degree. But when you're faced with keeping a roof over your head and food on the table, making money is your priority.

"Have you thought about going back?" he asks, pouring us both a glass of orange juice.

"I have. I'll probably look into it once I can save up some money and figure out where I'm going to settle." I smile.

Something flashes in his eyes, but I can't tell what. "You don't think you'll stay here?"

"I don't know. Not sure there's a reason to," I admit honestly. It's not like I've thought through leaving here, leaving him—whatever this is between us.

He takes a bite of his eggs, a sip of his orange juice, another bite of eggs, and he chews slowly. Finally, he asks me, "Where would you go?" His voice is quiet, as if he didn't really want to ask the question and doesn't want the answer.

"I've always dreamed of the Pacific Ocean. Maybe Oregon, in a small little town that sits on the edge of the ocean where I can walk the beach and breathe the cool air deep into my lungs." I smile at the thought. It's a beautiful picture, even if it never happens.

"Sounds nice," he says somberly.

"What about you? Ever think of leaving this place?" I wonder if he'd ever leave the only place he's ever called home.

"What, Arizona? Nah. The business is here. Really can't go anywhere else." Despite his words, I see his eyes spark with longing. The mood in the kitchen has suddenly shifted, and we both push the food around our plates. "But Oregon sounds really nice. I bet you'd love it there." He stands up abruptly and carries his plate to the sink. "I'll be in the office."

"Okay. I'm just going to clean up in here."

He nods at me and starts toward the office, then he stops. "Hey, Em?" My eyes meet his, and his smile is sincere. Somewhat sad, but sincere. "Oregon sounds amazing. If you ever get the chance, go."

I TWIST MY long, light brown hair into a messy bun and quickly run some lipstick over my lips. One last glance in the mirror, and I grab my wallet and phone off my nightstand. The house is still quiet, and I wonder what I've said or done to make Alex upset with me. He left brunch abruptly yesterday morning, and I haven't seen or heard from him since.

It's early, but Megan wants me there for the morning rush, so I scurry through the streets alongside the businessmen and women bustling to their jobs. As I push through the glass doors, Jax is wiping down a table.

"Good morning," I say with a big smile. It may sound weird, but I'm excited for today. Working has always been a source of pride for me, and I love staying busy.

"Morning, Emilia."

My name catches Megan's attention behind the counter, and she waves me over. "Ready for your first day?"

"I am. I'm excited." My clenching and unclenching hands prove it.

"Good. Let's get you settled." She shows me where I can put my wallet and phone under the counter, then she hands me a tan apron that has "Café Au Lait" printed across the front with a cup of cappuccino underneath it.

"This morning, just to get us through the rush, I'm going to have you plate or bag the baked goods and get any drip coffee that customers order. After the morning rush, I'll show you how to work the espresso machine and how we make some of our specialty coffees. Jax will handle ringing them up and any cold drink orders. We do have some iced teas and frappuccinos. Does that sound okay?"

I nod, pleased. "Sounds perfect."

"Good. I'm really excited you're working with us, Emilia. Brace yourself; it's about to get crazy." She laughs just as the front door opens and people start shuffling in.

The next three hours are non-stop madness. I restock the pastry case three different times, and Megan, Jax, and I actually work well together. I sneak out from behind the counter a couple times to wipe down tables and restock the bar with more sugar, creamer, and other condiments. Megan seems pleasantly surprised with my willingness to jump in and make sure things are taken care of.

As the morning rush finally diminishes, Jax and I do a more thorough cleaning of the seating areas.

"You did good this morning, sunshine," he says.

"Sunshine?" I cock an eyebrow at him and laugh.

"Yeah, you're always so happy, like the sunshine. It's my name for you."

"Well, thanks." Even though I don't know him well, the nickname warms me. "We're a good team."

"We are. It's nice to have someone who's on top of things. I can already tell Megan has a crush on you." He winks at me.

"She does not," I say laughingly.

"Em, not 'that' kind of crush." He rolls his eyes as if I'm totally naïve. "You're kick ass, and she's happy."

"Oh." I laugh out loud. "So, are the mornings always this busy?"

"Always. It'll quiet down now for a while. We get a few regulars that come in and do meetings, but it'll pick back up again around lunchtime until three o'clock."

"I kind of like when it's busy," I muse. "You don't even realize how fast time goes by."

He nods and whistles a tune to himself. "So, what's your story? Where are you from? What made you want to work at Café Au Lait?"

Questions like these always fluster me. I've never been one to lie, but I'm not ready to lay my sorry life out for others to judge me. "I just moved here from Illinois. My dad lives here. We're working at reestablishing a relationship." I shrug, hoping that appeases him, even though it's not true.

"Cool. So, you're a student?"

"Not right now. I plan to get back to school once I get settled and save up some money. What about you?" I want to divert the conversation to him.

"Well, Megan's my sister, and I help her run this place."

"What? You and Megan are related?" My eyes must bulge in disbelief.

He laughs. "We are. She's older and smarter and more gravitationally inclined to run a business. I'm younger and more carefree and don't like long-term commitments." He points to his curly hair that's pulled back into a bun and the small gauges in his ears.

"No wonder I didn't make the connection that you're related," I joke with him.

"Ah, I like your snark, sunshine."

Megan spends some time showing me around the espresso machine, and I make a few practice drinks under her watchful eye. Jax promises to show me how to work the register tomorrow as we finish up the last of our prep work for the next shift. The day passes quickly, and I'm thankful and content at the same time. I expected to see Sam today, but he didn't stop by. I chastise myself for feeling disappointed, but I was actually hoping to see him.

Hanging up my apron, I collect my wallet and phone from under the counter, then wave goodbye to Megan, who's in the back room at a tiny desk, doing paperwork and placing orders.

"Thanks again for everything, Jax. I'll see you tomorrow." I wave to him as I step out into the late afternoon sun. Holy hell, it's hot out here. I notice large clouds forming in the sky to the south over a large mountain range. As I walk the few blocks back to the condo, I keep an eye on the sky and the growing clouds. They're beautiful and ominous, and I'm absolutely fascinated by them. My mom and I would spend hours watching out the small windows of our trailer the impending thunderstorms that would roll through White Lake each summer. Lost in my memories, I'm shocked to find myself at the entrance to Alex's condo already.

"Hey, Fred!" I belt out as I walk past him and into a waiting elevator.

"Good afternoon, Ms. Adams," I hear him reply as the doors to the elevator close behind me.

The condo is quiet. No sign of Rosa, but the bowl of fresh

fruit and a freshly baked loaf of what looks like banana bread tells me she was here today.

"Rosa?" I holler, waiting for an answer that doesn't come. "Alex?" Again, no response.

I pull out my cellphone and type out a quick message to Alex. Minutes pass and still no response. I stand in the living room at the floor-to-ceiling windows and watch the large storm clouds continue to build and move closer. The sky is getting dark, and it reminds me again of how the thunderstorms would roll into town back in Illinois.

I step out onto the patio and watch the shrubs and trees begin to whip violently in the wind. The hot air blasts against my face, and the smell of dust stings my nose. The city ten stories below comes to a standstill as the afternoon storm rolls in. Cars disappear from the streets as the heavy rain falls in buckets. I stand at the edge of the patio looking out, the mountains no longer visible against the grayish brown sky.

"Emilia," Rosa yells from the patio door. "Get inside here before you get struck by lightning. What is wrong with you, *mija?*"

I push myself off the brick wall and head back into the house.

Rosa waits with her arms folded across her chest. "When did you get back?"

"Just a few minutes ago. I didn't think you were here."

"I had to run to the market." She points to the grocery bags on the kitchen island.

"Do you want some help?" I ask as I begin nosing through the bags.

"I'd love that." She perks up, the threat of getting struck by lightning forgotten, although it was nice to be thought of, to be warned. "I have to say, it's nice to have a girl around here to talk to."

"It's nice for me too," I say, pulling groceries from the reusable shopping bags and setting them on the counter as Rosa begins sorting and putting away. "Have you seen Alex today?" I ask, trying to sound nonchalant.

She glances at me briefly, carrying an armful of fruits and vegetables to the fridge. "Emilia." I love how my name rolls off her tongue with her thick Mexican accent. She clucks her tongue once in a motherly way. "It's really none of my business, but I feel like I should let you know that it's best not to ask questions about Alex's business."

"I didn't ask about his business. I asked if you'd seen him today," I say calmly. Why do people keep telling me this?

Rosa sighs. "Everything about that boy is his business. Here's what I can say. He will disappear for hours, days, and sometimes even a week or two. It is expected of us to not ask questions and just carry on. There may be times we see things or hear things, and we cannot let on that we did. We must keep our heads down and our noses in our own business."

I grit my teeth, growing irritable when she says, "He cares about you, though. If he's going to be gone, I'm sure he'll tell you."

"I'm his roommate. He doesn't have to tell me anything," I say sarcastically, immediately feeling bad for my snarky tone.

"You're more than a roommate. Don't let these living 'arrangements' fool you," Rosa informs me.

"What do you mean by that?" My heart beats rapidly as Rosa turns to me.

"He's never let another woman stay in this house. In fact,

very few women have spent more than an hour in this house." She raises her eyebrows and shakes her head. "You are not *just* a roommate."

"Then what am I?" It's the question of the day, the week, the big, thought-eating question that has haunted me since I met him, really.

She shakes her head at me and blows out a puff of air. "That's for you two to discuss."

Fine. Maybe we will. Because I'm tired of wondering.

With that decided, we finish unpacking the groceries in silence, and I go lie down for a bit while Rosa makes dinner. Before I fall asleep, I check my phone one last time in hopes that Alex responded. But he hasn't.

chapter nine
Alex

ONE THING I'VE learned in this business is: trust no one. So, I
shouldn't be surprised when Saul rolls up on my stash house on
Sunset Drive, and I see Manuel's head inside the driver's window
of a blacked-out seven series BMW. None of my guys drive
BMWs.

"Boss." Saul jumps to attention when he sees what I've
already noticed.

"Just keep driving. He doesn't know this car; he won't
recognize us," I advise Saul. "As we pass, take a good look and
see if you can ID who he's talking to."

"Yes, sir." Saul drives by, looking like he belongs in the
neighborhood with his pickup truck, and I slouch back in
my seat, hoping to go unnoticed. "I can't be sure, boss, but it
doesn't look like anyone on our radar. Pretty sure they were
black."

"Fuck!" I yell and punch the dashboard of his new pickup
truck.

"Want me to handle it?" He makes a right turn down another street.

"Pull over," I grumble. I'm fucking pissed that Manuel could be compromising my business with a potential street gang.

Saul pulls over to the curb, and we sit quietly while I contemplate what to do. "Who do we have watching Sunset?" I run through the list of my men that are accounted for and working.

"It was Rico, but now it's Manuel."

"So, he's alone?"

"*Si*. Rico is transferring goods today." By "goods," he means drugs, people—my business, my livelihood. Because I'm a fucking disgusting human being. I'm better than this, yet here I am.

"Okay. Turn around and go back."

Saul flips the truck into drive and makes a sharp U-turn. The wind has picked up from the impending monsoon, and lightning flits across the dark sky as we turn back onto Sunset Drive and toward my stash house.

"What's the plan, boss?"

The BMW is gone, and there's now no sign of Manuel. "Pull into the driveway and stay here. I'm going inside." And finding out what the fuck is going on.

He nods, and puts the truck in park. I pull out my phone and my gun, and head for the front door, which is wide open. Manuel is standing just inside, on the phone. I step to the side so he can't see me, and I listen to his conversation. What I hear has me fucking furious.

Without thinking, I slam the door closed behind me. "Manuel!"

He drops the phone. "Alejandro!" He eyes the gun in

my right hand.

"Hang it up." I nod toward the phone on the floor.

He swallows hard and bends down to retrieve the phone, shoving it in his pocket.

"Not so fast, hand it over."

"What?" He looks terrified.

"The phone. Hand it over."

He pulls the phone from his pocket and hands it to me.

"There's only one way to do this, Manuel."

"Do what?" he barks at me, becoming agitated.

"Find out what you're up to. You can tell me the truth, or I can call whoever it was you were just on the phone with."

He rakes his hands over his face. "It's nothing. Just a little side business."

"A little side business?" I see red and anger roils through my body.

He glances over to the stacked bundles of marijuana, and I notice one is cut open. "So you're funding your little side business with stolen weed?"

He shifts nervously, his eyes never leaving my gun.

"Answer me, goddammit!" I'm about to boil over with rage. I've never killed anyone in my life, but Manuel is damn close to becoming the first.

"Yes, I'm sorry. I just needed to bring in some extra cash…" He stands shorter than me, and sweat beads form along his forehead at his hairline. His dark eyes plead with me not to hurt him.

"You don't think we take care of you? You don't think we would've helped you out? No? So you steal from me? You fucking steal from me?" I raise my gun and shove it into his chest, knocking him off balance.

"I'm sorry, so fucking sorry, fuck, fuck," he stutters. "It won't happen again."

"You're damn right, it won't happen again." Just then, I hear the crack. My ear rings as the gunshot echoes through the otherwise empty house, and warm blood hits me across the face, catching me off guard.

Manuel falls to the ground and doesn't move. Blood pools around him from the gaping hole in his neck.

"Jesus Christ!" I swivel to see Saul standing behind me, his gun still pointed at Manuel. "Why did you shoot him?" I use the sleeve of my shirt to wipe the blood off my face.

Saul shrugs, like it's no big deal he just murdered someone. "He needed to be taken out. Your father would've wanted this."

"I am not my father," I grind out. "I'm running this organization now. Not him!" I vowed to run my father's business differently while he was in prison. I stalk over to the window and scan the area, hoping the shot and yelling hasn't attracted any neighbors. "We need to get out of here. It wouldn't surprise me if the police show up. Drop me off, and then come back and handle this."

I glance once at Manuel on the floor, lying in a pool of his own blood. My pulse quickens; I feel sick. The sight of blood always reminds me of my mother's death.

"Let's go," I bark at Saul.

I hate death, and I hate violence, yet this is my world. This is what I'm surrounded by now. I'm no longer the business major behind the finances, sitting in my small home office, playing with money. I'm running a fucking violent criminal organization. My heart races all the way back to the condo. No words are exchanged between Saul and me. I presume my balled up fists and heavy breathing are signal enough that I am fucking pissed.

"I want that cleaned up. And handle him appropriately," I tell him firmly. He nods at me as he pulls into the parking garage. "And if you ever pull a stunt like that again, it'll be *me* fucking blowing *your* head off. Do you understand?"

"Yes, sir." He grinds his jaw in annoyance with me.

"You take orders from me now, not my father. Things are handled differently, and you need to accept that."

"I will." I see his knuckles turning white as he grips the steering wheel. My father let Saul do whatever he wanted, and I won't have that. He's reckless and dangerous and a liability—but I have to keep him.

I slam the truck door behind me as Saul steps on the gas and peels down the parking garage. Stepping into the elevator, I catch the first glimpse of myself in the polished, stainless steel doors. "Fuck," I mutter at the blood splatter on my shirt and the blood that has dried on my face and neck.

The elevator opens, and I pause just outside my condo. I need a moment to collect myself before going inside. My stomach turns and I shove down the nausea, taking three deep breaths. Turning the handle, I step inside and hear Rosa and Emilia laughing and talking in the kitchen. There's no way to avoid them. Taking a deep breath, I enter the kitchen. Emilia is sitting on a stool at the island, eating dinner, and Rosa is across the counter, talking.

Rosa's face falls flat when she sees me, and I shake my head at her, telling her not to ask or say anything. Emilia must pick up on Rosa's shock and turns around. When her eyes find mine, they drop to my neck, then to my chest. Her fork clatters to the glass plate, and she lunges off the stool, toward me.

"Oh my God, what happened? Are you okay?" she cries.

I grab her by the upper arms to stop her. I don't want her touching me. "I'm fine." My words are clipped, and I can see the worry on her face, but I gently move her to the side and walk past her.

Rosa scurries around the kitchen counter and pulls Emilia to her as I make my way to my bedroom. I turn on the shower and strip my clothes, leaving them in a pile on the floor. They need to be burned, along with my shoes. Steam begins to billow out of the shower, and I take deep breaths of the hot steamy air. The sting of hot water against my skin is nothing compared to the ache I feel inside. Today, I was the cause of someone's death. I may as well have murdered him myself. With a washcloth doused with body wash, I scrub my skin, again and again. But no matter how hard I scrub, or how long I stand under this scalding water, I can still feel Manuel's warm blood on me. I can still see his dead, unseeing eyes. I can still see the hole in his neck, the blood pooling beneath him.

"Alex?" I hear her faint voice, although I can't see her through the steam-covered glass.

I press my forehead to the porcelain wall. I don't want her to see me like this. "Em, now's not a good time."

"I know," she says, small and shakily. "I just want you to know I'm here for you." She pauses. "When you're ready."

But will I ever be ready to tell her who I really am?

Shutting off the water, I pull a large towel from the rack. The cool air pricks at my skin as I step out of the steam and into the cool room. I dress in a pair of jeans and a light blue Polo t-shirt before fishing my cell phone out of the pocket of my other pants.

It makes me sick to my stomach again just looking at them. They're covered in sin.

Hovering over the call button, I finally get the courage to press it.

"Hello?" His voice is calm but cautious.

"I need to see you… tonight."

"I'll be waiting." His voice is concerned, but I trust he'll be waiting for me.

The phone disconnects, and I sit at the edge of my bed, head bowed. It takes a few minutes before I'm ready to leave my room, but finally, I venture out. The house is quiet. Rosa is gone by now, and Emilia's door is wide open, but she's not inside. As I head down the hallway, I finally see her sitting in the middle of the living room floor. She's perched on the plush throw rug that sits between the couch and a large wood table that I had made for this room.

For a long minute, I stand and watch her. She's hunched over, painting her toes with slow, methodical strokes. Her long hair is tied, and her cheeks are flushed pink. Just the sight of her relaxes me. Amazing how she can do that. I don't understand it, and I don't understand how I've gone this long in my life without her as a sort of life source. I already feel my heart rate returning to normal, that sick feeling in my stomach dissipating.

Everything about her is sweet. Pure. Innocent. She is why I want to change. She makes me want to be a man that she deserves, that she can find happiness with and give her the dreams she so badly deserves. Everything I've never felt for anyone else, I feel for her.

I swallow hard as she blows a stray strand of hair from her face and rocks back on her butt, wiggling her toes as they dry. My lips pull into a small smile. I could watch her for hours, maybe days, and never be bored. She is perfection.

Finally, she catches me watching and shoots a cautious smile at me. She remains rooted in place—no words exchanged between us—just a sympathetic look. She's giving me the space I asked for, but all I want is to lose myself inside her.

"Come with me," I say quietly.

"Where?" I see the hesitation in her eyes. The fear. Fuck, I came home covered in another man's blood—she should be horrified—but yet, she's still here. She watches me tentatively, but something passes between us—a look of trust.

"Just walk with me."

She pushes herself up and slides her feet into a pair of flip-flops, setting the small bottle of nail polish on the table. I reach for her hand. She takes it, but not before pulling me into a hug. She holds on to me for dear life, yet I don't have the courage to hug her back. She senses my tension and pulls away, her eyes cast downward at her feet. I hate that I push her away when I need her most, but mostly I hate that I can't return the affection that she deserves.

We walk hand in hand through the quiet downtown streets to the only place I seem to find myself when my life is falling apart. The church comes into view, and Em squeezes my hand as we turn the corner and make our way across the street.

Standing in front, she suddenly pulls her hand from mine. "Go. I'll be waiting right here."

Like hell. "No. I don't like you out here by yourself."

"Alex." Her tone is firm. "I said I'll be fine. Go."

She's fierce and independent and won't be told no—a few of her qualities that I simultaneously love and hate. As much as I want to force her inside, I respect her confidence and ability to push back. After a moment, I nod and turn away from her, heading inside. By myself.

Father Mark is in the front pew, his head bowed in prayer. The aisle is long and the church is mostly dark, with the exception of some dim lights that illuminate the Stations of the Cross lining the perimeter.

At the sound of my shoes on the old wood floor, Father Mark turns around and gestures for me to come forward, and I slide into the pew next to him.

"What's bothering you, Alejandro?"

Emotions bubble just under the surface. Emotions I've never felt comfortable dealing with, so I've shoved them down. Buried them beneath the hate, the anger, the sadness that is my life. But now they bubble, coming up so high that my throat tightens, and I feel tears begin to form in my eyes. The last time I cried was when I watched my mom be lowered into the ground and covered in dirt. I wasn't allowed to cry after that. My dad wouldn't allow tears. I sit quietly, not knowing where to even begin.

"Take all the time you need, Alejandro," Father Mark says, giving me the time I need to form words.

I swallow hard against the lump in my throat and focus on the stained-glass window just behind Father Mark. I'm too much of a coward to look him in the eye.

"I killed a man today." I can almost hear him gasp, but he sits silently. "Not with my own hands, but indirectly." He nods slowly, but doesn't speak. "I can't do this anymore—I never wanted to do it in the first place," I choke out. A lone tear falls from the corner of my eye, and I quickly bat it away.

"Alejandro…" He pauses. "You always have a choice."

I shake my head. I don't have a choice. In this life, this business, there are no choices. Your choices are made for you. This is how the family business works.

"They'll kill me, Father. There is no choice. I stay or I die. That's it."

He takes that in and stares up at the intricate peeks in the ceiling. "Do you remember when you first started to come and see me? After your mom passed?"

"Yeah." Father Mark was the only person in the world I could talk to. He listened and comforted me in the years after my mom passed. He doesn't judge me, even though he knows I'm a horrible person.

"You'd walk across the street from the school and come into the parish, and sit in the pew, and just stare at the altar."

Those days are so ingrained in my memory. I remember every detail. The wooden pews, the altar, the smell—this church has always brought me peace and comforted me. Nothing has changed here from twenty years ago. "I remember."

"I was so sad to see you here. As much I loved our time talking about your mother and your school, I hurt for you. Your brother got lucky, and you got the short end of the stick. I was so angry at your father for not letting you go with them. Your aunt and uncle were willing to take both of you, but your father marked you. He wanted you in the business, and there was no convincing him otherwise. I tried, Alex. I tried so hard to convince him to let them take you both." Father Mark hangs his head in sorrow, a feeling I am very familiar with.

Then he wrings his hands together and stares at the pulpit in front of us. "All I could do then was pray for you. Pray you'd continue to come and see me, and pray that God would watch over you and protect you. All these years, you've kept coming, and all these years, I've been guiding you and praying that one day you'd stop coming because you had made the conscious decision to get out, to get away from all of this. But every Sunday, you sit in that pew." He points to the back of the church. "And every Saturday, you come for confession."

He leans forward and hangs both of his arms over the pew, lacing his fingers together. "I long for the day that I walk into this church and you're not here… but not because you've become a victim to this life… but because you chose to get out."

As I listen to Father Mark, I suddenly realize that this is the only place I've ever felt safe.

"Remember after mass on Sunday when I pulled you aside?" he continues, a desperate glint in his eyes. "I told you that you had to do right by Emilia. Be truthful with her. This is your opportunity to go. Take her and go. Get away from this."

I feel all of his words, and I want what he wants. I have wanted that for so long, but I feel so fucking helpless. "It's not that easy."

"Nothing in life that matters is." He stands up and looks at me. "Let's not forget your penance, son. Two Hail Mary's, and I want you to visit your mother. Talk to her."

"She's dead." My voice breaks as her memory floods my mind.

"I know this. Visit her gravesite." He begins to walk away. "And there's someone waiting for you." He gestures to the back of the church. I turn slowly to see Emilia sitting silently in the last pew.

"Goodnight, Alejandro."

"Night, Father."

I compose myself before heading back to her.

"Hi," she says with a small, hopeful smile.

"Hi." God, she looks beautiful, and I want to hold her. I want to touch her. I want to let go and run away from this fucking horrible life and be with her and give her the world.

"Feel better?"

"A little." I shrug and take her hand. Just her warm palm in mine clenches the walls around my heart. A small sense of hope finds its way inside of me and roots itself. As we leave, I turn back and see Father Mark watching us. He offers a tight smile and a nod before we disappear into the humid Phoenix night.

I CHECK THE business accounts one last time to ensure today's deposits were made, and I check emails to make sure tomorrow's delivery from Mexico is still on schedule as planned. I make sure all the security cameras are on and working before shutting down for the evening.

Emilia is sound asleep and curled up in a ball on the sectional in the game room, with the TV remote in her hand. Pulling a blanket from the back of the couch, I lay it over her body. "*Buenos noches, mi amor*," slips from my lips as I kiss her forehead gently and turn off the TV. I've never called anyone "my love" before—until Emilia.

For the next hour, I toss and turn until I feel the bed shift behind me. Emilia's warm body slides under the covers, and she wraps herself around me. I pull her hand to my chest, and we lie in the silent dark. She's comforting me the only way I'll let her—without words. After a while, I feel her pulling away, but I hold on to her, not letting her go.

"Alex, I need to go to bed. I have to work in the morning."

"Just stay for a minute. I need to talk to you." I feel her body stiffen before she relaxes back into me. We're both on our backs, our fingers laced tightly together in the pitch black room. I struggle with how to tell her who I am and what I do. I know she can sense my nervousness.

"It's bad, isn't it?" Her voice is feeble.

"It is," I admit honestly.

She squeezes my hand, urging me to begin. Lying next to her in the dark, I feel less vulnerable. Like if she can't see me exposing myself, maybe it'll hurt me less because I won't be able to see her disappointment—her disgust.

"Everything you think you know about me is a lie. I run the Estrada drug cartel." I swear she stops breathing. There is no sound or movement coming from her. "Em? Say something."

"You sell drugs?" she whispers.

Shit. "Well, I don't sell them... but my family's business imports them from Mexico, and we distribute them to people who do sell them."

She snorts and pulls away slightly, creating some distance between us on the bed, but I won't let go of her hand. I'm not letting her run away from me. "Imports. I like how you put that little spin on it. These are drugs, Alex, not Persian rugs. You import drugs. You *smuggle* them into the country."

I grip her hand tighter as she tries to pull away further.

"Is there anything else?"

"Yeah." I swallow hard.

142

"God," she mumbles under her breath.

"We also smuggle guns and people."

"Jesus Christ, you're a trafficker?" She's horrified and rightfully so. "It all makes sense now. The security, the cameras, the paranoia… the blood. Oh God, did you hurt someone today? Please tell me you didn't—"

I cut her off. "I didn't. Someone else did."

"Alex, why? Why you?" Her voice is pained.

"I ask myself that same question every fucking day. It's all I know, Em. I was raised in this business. I fucking hate it, though. It's what killed my mother, took my brother away from me, yet here I am."

"So, tell your father you're done," she begs. "Let him manage the business. You said you have a business degree—you can do anything with that."

"I can't. It doesn't work that way. You can't just walk away from a cartel. I know too much. If I'm not actively involved in the organization, then I'm a liability to the organization. Do you know what they do to liabilities? They kill them, no questions asked. No remorse. That's why I want you to know nothing. I don't want you in the middle of this, Emilia. I shouldn't have even told you this. I care too much about you."

"Talk to your father, reason with him. He has to understand that you deserve better than this. He's your *father*!"

I laugh without humor. My father can't be reasoned with. It's his way or no way, and he's going to be pissed enough that I've not followed "his way" of operating this business. However, I've kept us under the radar, we're moving supply, and the money is coming in. Most importantly, no one has died—except for

Manuel. But that's because Saul was managing under my father's "way."

"He's not reasonable. Plus, he's in jail right now. The feds are breathing down our throats. I've got the FBI, the DEA, and ATF watching our every move. Most of our guys have gone missing or are dead... and the entire organization is hinging on me right now. I'm holding all of it together." I squeeze her hand again, to keep myself grounded and to keep her from fleeing.

I can't believe I'm telling her all of this. I'm baring my soul to Emilia and she's listening. She's trusting me with the truth. I can feel her hand shaking in mine, but we remain silent. We lie for minutes. She won't let go. Her sniffles tell me she's crying, but I'm too much of a coward to even comfort her right now.

"Why did you stop to help me?" Her voice shakes as she asks me this, and those few words threaten to break me. It would break me completely if she thought there was no good in me, nothing worth saving.

"Because I could tell you needed someone. Because I just wanted to do something *good* for once." My voice cracks around "good." "When I see you, all I see is good, Em. I'm so sorry I brought you into the middle of this. It was selfish of me." *So fucking selfish.*

"I'm not sorry, Alex," she says, her voice passionate. "Let's go away together, just you and me. We'll go somewhere obscure. North Dakota or Montana. No one will look there. We'll figure it out once we get there."

How great would that be? It'll never happen. "Em," I cut her off. "I can't. I wish I could be what you need, what you deserve. I want more than anything to disappear with you, and I wish I could give you all your dreams... but I can't. I had just a little taste of you, and I got greedy and took more. I shouldn't have done that. You deserve better than what I can give you… which is just this."

I swallow hard and my heart falls into my stomach. After everything I've just confessed, she still wants me. Yet, I know all I'll ever do is hurt her. I loosen the hold on her hand, but she leaves her palm resting on top of mine. Her sniffles slow, but I know she's not asleep because we're both restless. As the sun begins to rise, and the slightest hint of orange sky peeks through my window, she slips out of my bed and leaves. My heart hurts, screams for me to bring her back and keep her here… but I let her walk away.

Heavily, I get out of bed and pull an Adidas duffle bag from my closet. Dressing quickly, I stuff the bag with enough clothes to last me a week, then I lift the picture off the wall and open the hidden safe in my room, pulling out a bundle of cash—pre-counted, ten thousand dollars. I count out two thousand and set it aside, shoving the other eight into my bag.

In the kitchen, Rosa eyes my duffle bag. I grab an apple from the fruit bowl and a bottle of water out of the fridge. Tossing the cash on the counter, I point at it. "For Emilia."

She nods but doesn't ask questions. Rosa's been around long enough to know sometimes you don't want the answers to questions, so she's stopped asking.

"I'm going to Mexico."

Her eyes widen, and she shakes her head at me, but doesn't say anything.

"Emilia knows everything," I tell her.

"And?" Rosa's eyes are full of hope, and I see right through her. She wanted Emilia to be it, the one that saves me from this life.

"And I don't know," I tell her, keeping my voice devoid of emotion. "I don't know what she's thinking. If she's gone when I get back, I wouldn't be surprised." Rosa wipes her hands on a kitchen towel before folding it and putting it on the counter.

Her expression turns motherly, and it's all I can do to keep standing. "Please be safe, *mijo*."

"I will. Please watch her." I nod toward Emilia's room.

"She loves you, you know."

"I know." I swallow hard against my dry throat, but I don't look back.

The door closes behind me, and I'm already on my way down the elevator when I wonder if Emilia walking out of my room this morning will be the last time I ever see her.

chapter ten

Emilia

ROSA LOOKS UP with a worried face when I finally emerge from my bedroom. No matter how much concealer I put on, it does nothing to erase the dark circles from my eyes.

"Coffee?" she asks.

"That would be wonderful. Thanks." I slide onto one of the barstools and rest my elbows on the counter. I press my fingertips into my temples, rubbing them aggressively, trying to relieve my pounding headache.

"Here." She slides the steaming mug across the granite countertop. "Give me your hand." She pulls my hand into hers and begins massaging different spots on it. It hurts and feels amazing all at the same time. "There are pressure points in your hand," she explains, squeezing and holding another spot. "When you massage them, it's supposed to help with headaches."

I lift the mug of coffee with my other hand and take a sip. "I heard him leave," I say softly, and she freezes. "I heard him say he's going to Mexico. How long will he be gone?"

"I don't know, *mija*." She shakes her head sadly. "Weeks? Days?"

"Why is he going to Mexico?" My stomach flips when I ask this. I know why he's going to Mexico. Drugs. Guns. Human smuggling. Never in the furthest reaches of my brain did I expect Alex to tell me he runs a drug cartel. But what puzzles me more is the fact that he's shared his truth, a truth I've accepted, and I still need him. Still want him.

She sighs. "I presume business, but I don't ask."

"Does he go often?"

She shakes her head. "No. He rarely goes to Mexico, Emilia." She pauses. "I don't know how to say this nicely, but please don't go digging. You know too much already. The less you know, the better." She picks up a bottle of cleaner and sprays the kitchen island, wiping it clean with a towel.

"I'm not afraid of him." I don't know why I say that, but I want her to know that what he's revealed isn't going to scare me away. From the very first time I met him at that dingy motel, I felt drawn to him. He was safe to me when I felt unsafe, like he was put in my path for a reason.

She turns to look at me, and I can see the fear in her dark eyes. "It's not Alejandro you need to be afraid of. That boy would never hurt you. It's everyone else." Her voice carries an air of warning. "Be very careful of what you say and who you talk to, Emilia. I'm serious." She pats my hand before disappearing down the hall with a basket of laundry on her hip.

Phone and wallet in hand, I walk the four short blocks to Café Au Lait. Even though it's bright and sunny, the downtown Phoenix streets are deserted. In less than an hour, this'll be a bustling metropolis once again, but right now, the streets are eerily quiet. I find myself glancing over my shoulder, more aware of my surroundings. I take the time to look down alleys as I cross them instead of staring at the cracked sidewalks like I used to. Being with Alex has changed me, made me somewhat paranoid. And yet I still wouldn't change it. He is my safe place.

The door to Café Au Lait is locked, but Jax sees me and jogs over to let me in. "Mornin'," he says, his attitude upbeat. "No offense, but you look like hell. Everything okay?"

I place my belongings on the shelf and grab my apron. "Yeah. Unfortunately for me, when I don't sleep well, I look like I've taken a few good punches to both eyes." I smile at him and tie the strings of the apron around my waist.

"Well, you're working in the right place for a little pick me up." He laughs. "I'll make you a cappuccino if you want to stock the case with fresh pastries. The delivery just came in."

"That sounds like an amazing plan." I sigh loudly, then go find Megan, who is sitting at her desk working on paperwork as I pull two boxes of pastries from the wire shelves. "Good morning, Megan."

"Morning, Emilia. Those were just delivered. Still waiting on the muffins…" The words are just out of her mouth when there's a knock on the back delivery door. Megan rolls her chair over and peeks through the peephole before opening the door. "We were just talking about you." She smiles at the delivery man.

"Sorry I'm late," the old man says as he shoves three boxes of muffins at Megan. She sets them on the counter and signs his papers before he scurries away quickly, obviously late for all of his deliveries.

"That was Martin." She laughs. "He's always late and *always* overfriendly," she says with an eye roll, alluding to his lack of friendliness.

"I'll come back for the muffins in a minute. Let me get these in the case first."

She smiles at me and rolls back to her desk. Her fingers begin pounding away on her keyboard before I even get out of the back room. Jax is filling stainless steel containers with milk and creamer, and stocking the station with extra napkins, stir sticks, and sugar.

"There's an envelope on the counter for you, Emilia. It's your tips from yesterday. Sorry I forgot to give it to you before you left." I pick up the thick envelope and stick it under the counter with my phone and wallet.

I stock the glass case with the pastries and muffins, and then Jax shows me how to make the various drip coffees. "Not everyone is an espresso drinker." He smirks. "We usually have our signature roast, which is a medium blend. Not too strong, not too light. It's our best seller. We grind all the beans here; keeps it fresh."

Jax is patient when he shows me how to measure the right amount of beans, pour them into the grinder, and set the large drip coffee machines to start. "Keep an eye on this," he says as he points to a small level on the side. "It'll tell you when we're getting low on coffee and when to make more. We do *not* want to run out of this." He laughs, and we work side by side, making the other three blends. A light roast, a dark roast, and today's specialty flavor—cinnamon.

"Sunshine, you're a natural here. Seriously. No one has picked up on the ins and outs so quickly. You just get it."

"Aw, thanks." I smile and give him a little exaggerated curtsy.

Jax tips his head back and laughs openly at me. "Go ahead and unlock the door, let's get this party started." He turns on the overhead music, and I unlock the front doors.

Not a minute later, the first customer walks in and, from there, the morning rush begins. Jax and I manage the front by ourselves for the first hour before Megan peeks out from the back office. "I swear you were an answer to my prayers." She nudges me gently with her hip and smiles as she puts on an apron. "If I didn't know better, I'd think you were trying to take over my business."

"Hardly, but I really like it here, Megan." And it's the truth. "Thank you for taking a chance on me."

She shoots me a sympathetic smile. "Good, because you're never allowed to quit." I'm so thankful to have this job.

We spend the next hour working much like we did yesterday—in unison. As the morning rush winds down and I'm refilling the canisters of creamer and milk, the front door opens and Sam saunters in. In a dark gray suit and white dress shirt, he's every bit as handsome as the last time I saw him.

"Emilia." He smiles at me and nervously shoves his hands into the front pockets of his pants.

"Hi, Sam." I catch Jax wagging his eyebrows at me, and I stifle a laugh. Sam looks over his shoulder at Jax, who pretends to be busy wiping down the counter. "Can I get you a coffee or something to eat?"

"Coffee would be great. Any chance you could join me for a few minutes?"

"Yeah, I think I can arrange that. Go grab a table. I'll get you a coffee."

He rocks back on his heels before turning around to find a

table. I see him pick a high-top in the back corner, away from the other patrons.

I grab two cups, filling one with the dark roast for Sam and one with today's special for me. "Hey, Jax, mind if I take a few minutes?"

"Take your time." He winks at me. I juggle the two coffees and a handful of creamers and sugars over to the table.

Sam grabs one of the coffees for me. "So, how are you liking the new job?" he asks as I settle into my chair.

"I like it. I can't believe how fast the days pass. This place is always busy."

"I told you, best coffee in town," he says with a smirk.

"That's what everyone says. How's work been for you? You said you've been busy when I saw you on Sunday." Sam flashes me a sincere smile and rubs his square jaw.

"Really busy." He nods. "I wanted to stop by yesterday to see how your first day was, but I just couldn't get away."

"Thanks for thinking of me." I drop my eyes. Very few men have ever shown an interest in me before Alex, and I blush at his sincerity. "So, what exactly do you do? Banker?"

He shakes his head as he blows on his coffee. Taking a small sip, he carefully sets it back down on the table and his fingers strum the wood top. He tilts his head, looking around the coffee shop before turning back to me. Then he lowers his voice, not that anyone is around to hear him. It must be out of habit. "I work for the government."

"Seriously? So, like what do you do?" I'm genuinely interested.

Sam's cell rings, and he pulls it from the pocket of his suit jacket. "Excuse me. I need to take this really quick. Cortez," he says quietly.

I fold my hands into my lap to keep them from shaking as Sam watches me intently while he talks on the phone.

A moment later, he shoves his phone back into his jacket and grimaces. "The office. I have to get back, but I was wondering if you wanted to have dinner with me tonight?" His eyes twinkle with hope.

My stomach flips, and I can feel myself blush. "I can't."

"You can't or you won't?" He looks at my suspiciously.

"Can't." I smile at him and slide out of the chair. "And it sounds like you're insanely busy at work."

"I always have time to eat." He stands up, and we walk together toward the entrance.

"Maybe another time. It was nice talking to you." I hope I'm letting him down gently. I want to have dinner with Sam. I like Sam, but I love Alex.

"It was nice talking to you too, Emilia." His lips form a perfect smile, and his hazel eyes twinkle in the lights of the coffee shop. There's something about Sam that's comforting. I watch him disappear down the street before I return back behind the counter to help Jax with the new rush of people.

As the afternoon quiets down and Jax and I finish our prep for the next shift, my mind wanders back to Alex. I've checked my phone every hour, hoping for a text or a voicemail, and am disappointed to find nothing.

My mind is reeling with worry, knowing he's in Mexico.

"What's got your wheels turning, sunshine?" Jax asks quietly as he sidles up next to me. He scratches his short beard and raises his eyebrows. "You've been scrubbing that same spot on the counter for the last ten minutes."

I shake my head and sigh.

"And did you know that when you're deep in thought, you purse your lips and squint your eyes?" he asks.

"I do not," I argue, frowning.

"Sunshine, you do. Now what's got you so distracted and not sleeping? You look like hell."

I let out another deep sigh and look away. "Just have a lot on my mind right now."

"Well, I'm here if you ever want to talk. I've been told I'm a good listener."

"Thanks. I might take you up on that." I reach out and squeeze his forearm.

Changing the subject, Jax leans on the counter. "So, do you want to tell me about that Sam guy?"

"What about him?" I ask questioningly.

"Well, from the looks of the women that eye him every time he comes in here, he's one of Phoenix's most eligible bachelors. You've been in this place all of two days and he's taken a liking to you."

I snort. I actually snort at this observation. "I stepped on him!" I giggle. "When I was coming in to drop off my application, we were in line together, and I stepped on him. I was so embarrassed, Jax." I place my hand over my neck as I feel the flush begin to spread. "He ended up buying me a coffee, and we talked for a minute before Megan came over to interview me."

"Uh-huh." He winks at me. "And clearly, he was smitten."

"He's nice. I've only talked to him for a few minutes, but I'm impressed. He's clearly ambitious, has a good career—"

"What does he do?" Jax inquires.

"Not sure. He said he works for the government."

Jax nods. "Ah, I think he's one of those federal guys. He's been coming in almost every day for a few years. Like clockwork, he gets the dark roast. Creature of habit, predictable. I like that quality in people."

"Federal guys?" I ask as Jax sorts cash from the register. I'm curious and digging for information.

"I think it's something law enforcement related." He shrugs casually. "I've seen his badge before when he pulled out his wallet. Just didn't know exactly what kind. Probably an investigator with the IRS." He laughs, then counts the bills under his breath.

"He asked me to dinner," I admit as Jax fills the large metal iced tea dispenser.

Jax raises both eyebrows. "And..."

"And I don't know. I said I can't." *Because I love Alex.*

Jax frowns, confused. "Is there a reason you shouldn't go to dinner with him?"

I let out a nervous chuckle. "Is that your way of asking if I'm single?"

Jax laughs out loud. I love how our friendship is developing. I can tell he's someone I can trust. I've had so few of those in my life; it's a comforting feeling. "Not really. I'm more of a 'let's be direct with each other' kind of guy... but sure. Are you single?" he asks nervously and stills as he waits for me to answer.

I feel myself starting to squirm. "It's complicated." *Understatement of the century.*

Jax lets out a long, dramatic sigh. "You and half the people on Facebook are in a complicated relationship."

"I'm not in a relationship, I don't think. That's why it's complicated." I want to be in a relationship with Alex more than anything, but I heard his words loud and clear last night when he said he couldn't offer me anything more than sex, and my heart hurts. I never expected anything to happen with Alex, but like the tornado that he is, he pulled me into his storm and uprooted me. And just like a treacherous storm, he's shaken me with his truths and abandoned me when he left this morning.

"You don't *think* you're in a relationship?" Now he's thoroughly confused.

"No, I don't think so."

"So, you don't really know?"

"Right."

"Jesus, you're complicated." He shakes his head at me and chuckles. "Well, if it's that complicated, then having dinner with Loverboy isn't such a bad thing, you know? Maybe it'll bring some clarity to your *situation*." He says that last word with a hint of sarcasm, then laughs again and stands.

"Yeah, maybe," I mutter, although I don't think anything will bring clarity right now.

"Sunshine, I wish I had your complications."

"Do you have lady problems, Jax?" I turn the tables on him.

"More like lack of lady problems." He sighs lightly and shakes his head, dropping the subject and continuing on with work.

Jax hums as we finish the afternoon rush. The day has flown by just as it did yesterday. Megan spends most of her time working in the back office, since Jax and I have the front handled. I make a point of glancing out the front window every hour or so, and Andres hasn't moved once today. As I'm wiping down the counter, I smile at Jax's assessment of Sam.

"Look, go home and get some rest. I'll finish up here."

"Are you sure?"

"Yes! Here." He hands me another envelope. "Today's tips."

I untie my apron and hang it up before collecting my belongings. "I'll see you in the morning."

"Have a good one, Sunshine!"

I should turn right, but my feet take me left. Heat from the scorching pavement seeps through my flat sandals, and I can almost feel the soles of my feet begin to burn as I walk quickly through downtown Phoenix. It's late afternoon, and the sun is as hot as ever. The tall palm trees provide little shade as I walk briskly toward my destination.

My long legs take the steps at the large church two at a time. I stop to catch my breath at the top of the stairs. Gathering myself, I pull open one of the large wooden doors and step inside. It's dark with just the sun shining through the stained-glass windows. There's one light over the altar, illuminating the large crucifix behind it.

The church is quiet. No one is here, so I walk slowly down the long aisle, my fingers brushing the top of each pew. Sliding into one near the front, I sit quietly, a million thoughts and emotions bubbling at the surface.

I've never been a spiritual person, but there's no denying the presence I feel here. I stare at the large crucifix in front of me. It reminds me of the one Alex wears around his neck. At that, I close my eyes and think of him, tears burning under my closed eyelids. How can a person be so good to me and still be the person he claims to be?

A tear slips out, and I swat it away, soaking in the comfort of the church. I spend a few minutes praying to a God I'm still not sure exists, or is even listening to me.

"Emilia?" Even though the voice is gentle, I still startle.

"Father Mark." I exhale loudly. "You scared me."

He chuckles. "I'm sorry. I was surprised to see anyone in here."

"I hope it's okay I stopped by? I think I just needed to be here." *To clear my head, if that's even possible.*

"You're always welcome here," he says, his face so kind. "Mind if I sit down with you?"

"Please." I scoot over a bit, and he slides in next to me.

"What's bothering you, child?"

Child... I forget ever being a child. To be carefree and innocent. "You're the second person to ask me that today. Is it that obvious?"

"Emilia, you're crying. And most people don't show up here in the afternoon for a simple visit. They're usually reflecting or giving their problems to God."

"If only it were so easy to just give your problems to God." I snicker.

"Emilia. It *is* as easy as giving your problems to God. He won't be able to fix them, but he'll certainly guide you and show you how."

I contemplate his words.

As I'm in my thoughts, he says, "Tell me what's bothering you, child."

Those traitorous tears are back and quickly filling my eyes. I feel my lips shake and my chin quiver as I try to form words. After several failed attempts, I just shake my head, and he squeezes my hands, which are folded in my lap.

"When you're ready, I'll be here."

I nod, bury my face in my hands, and sob—loud, painful,

breath-stealing sobs. I sense Father Mark quietly leave, and I lean forward to rest my arms on the pew in front of me. I silently pray to God to show me, guide me, and offer me some direction. Raising my head, I stare at the statue of the Virgin Mary that sits in front of me, her arms open and welcoming. The church begins to get darker as the sun retreats in the sky. With a sigh, I stand to leave, but not before I whisper another quiet prayer.

As I turn, I notice Andres in the very back pew, not even attempting to hide himself. Not that he could. As I head down the aisle toward the door, he keeps his eyes turned down, but noiselessly stands as I pass him.

"Let's go, big guy," I mutter as I exit out into the sweltering Phoenix night. I glance back at the church once as I amble away, Andres on my heels. Today was a first for me. I gave my problems to God. Now let's see if he can figure out what I should do, because I sure as hell can't.

chapter eleven
Alex

You know you're in Mexico when the smell of exhaust burns your nose. As I maneuver this pickup truck through the pothole-riddled streets, I glance warily at the rundown concrete buildings doubling as bars, neon lights flashing signs for Modelo and Bud Light. I'm on my way to meet a business partner about a shipment of guns we have lined up for delivery, but this piece of shit pickup does little to disguise me in this small town in northwestern Sonora. Everyone knows everyone here, and I'm the outsider.

Men stand on street corners and hold their stare as I drive slowly through the streets, scanning the area for the building I'm meeting Navarro at. There are no building numbers to guide me. All I know is it's a teal building with a Tecate billboard above it.

Dust kicks up from the gravel street as I turn the steering wheel quickly, finally spotting the building. Juan Santiago and Alvaro pull up in a truck next to me. They work for my father here in Mexico and will ensure my safety while I'm here. As a habit, I make note of my surroundings before I exit the truck and approach the steel door. I nod at a local who's made it his business to let me know he's watching me, and he turns and goes back to whatever he was tending to.

I inhale a deep, calming breath before tugging the heavy door open. Inside, it looks like any other dive bar. Tall, beat-up pub tables are scattered throughout the sparse room. A few pool tables line the wall to the left with lights flickering over them—a sign of Mexico's still badly managed utility infrastructure.

"Estrada," the deep voice calls out from a corner booth behind me. When I turn, I see Navarro, flanked by two women—prostitutes, I assume. Empty shot glasses and beer bottles line the table, and I can make out the red, burning light of a cigarette.

"Navarro," I say as I approach the table. He reaches out his hand to shake mine and nods for me to take a seat across from him.

Juan Santiago takes a seat at the bar to watch us, and Alvaro stands near the entrance. They're good. They position themselves away from each other, but where they can easily watch everything happening inside.

"Ladies, Alejandro Estrada." Navarro introduces me with excitement in his voice.

I swallow hard and nod politely, barely containing my cringe when I see the bruises lining the inner arm of one of the women, a telltale signs that she's a junkie. Both women are dressed provocatively and hanging on each of his arms. I feel simultaneously disgusted and sympathetic toward them, but I hide it. I hide it all, keeping my face professional, powerful; exactly the façade I need to have while I'm here, even though I'm tired of this charade.

"Navarro, thanks for meeting me on such short notice."

"Is there a problem, son?"

"No, but we need to move back the shipment and change the route of the AKs. ATF is all over my ass, and I'm sure they've got our route marked. They're waiting to take this shipment out." Cortez and his men have been everywhere. The nice thing is they make their presence known. They don't hide. They want me and my business and they're brazen about taking it.

He nods as he licks his lips. "We can manage that. We'll come through Texas instead. Will take us longer to get them to you, but it's safer, I agree. It'll cost more, you know." He narrows his eyes slightly, an unspoken understanding that I'll have to pay.

I nod firmly. "I'm willing to pay. My buyers understand there will be a slight delay."

"Then let me make a few calls. How long will you be in Mexico?" the old man asks with a raspy voice. He reminds me of my father but heavier with short graying hair and dark sullen eyes.

"Not long. Tending to a few things, then I need to get back to Phoenix."

"How are you managing? I know things are tough right now." He glances at a man that stands with his elbow propped on the bar. I presume it's one of his men.

I sigh loudly, but don't want to let on that shit is bad. Navarro knows; he's testing me. "We're doing good. Shipments have been coming in—"

"Of all kinds?" he interrupts me, meaning drugs, guns—humans.

"Yes."

"Good. And you're turning them quickly?"

He watches me closely, and I keep my face neutral. The girls giggle with each other, paying no attention to us. "We are. We never hold on to goods long. We get them out of our hands, into the buyers'. Safest way to do business."

"Smartest way, son." He nods, pleased. "Your father was right about you. I'm proud of you."

Bile rises in my throat as he says this. Nothing could be further from the truth. I hate this business. I'd drive it into the fucking ground if I could. Honestly, I'm damn near tempted to, but I fake a smile and nod once again.

"Thank you." It's all I can say right now without showing how sick I feel.

"So, let me call you tomorrow after I make a few calls."

"Sounds good." I reach across the table and offer the man my hand once more, a sign of respect and thanks.

He's doing me a huge favor, and he didn't have to. I slide out of the booth, feeling every eye on me as I approach the exit. I can't help but wonder who works for whom, or who is a lookout for other organizations and how fast word will spread that I'm in town. Being at the top of the Estrada Cartel and running the show, I'm a target. The head they want severed and delivered to our rivals, and, if delivered, I'm the body that would bring our organization down.

It's dark when I start the truck and head back toward my dad's ranch on the outskirts of town. Juan Santiago and Alvaro are following closely behind me. We're a little over an hour from the border, but it feels like the heart of Central Mexico. I drive cautiously down the bumpy street, careful not to hit stray dogs or call attention to my vehicle. The drive to the ranch takes about twenty minutes, and I'm happy to see the security Dad has in place is still there. It's more of a compound than a ranch. With high stucco walls and decorative wrought iron that doubles as security fencing, it stands out in a town where dilapidated houses are the norm.

I pull up to the gate and roll down my window. Rogelio sweeps the truck before letting me through with a curt nod, and I park the truck next to my SUV, stepping down onto the cobblestone driveway. Rogelio stands outside the gate with a semi-automatic rifle propped on his shoulder as the gates slowly close. Small landscape lights illuminate the palm trees in the front yard. The landscape is manicured to perfection, another thing my dad set in place, even from jail.

Even with him in Federal custody, life in Mexico seems to continue as if he's a free man. No one misses a beat. The house is tidy and his housekeeper keeps food in the fridge and the pantry. Security is tight, and the Mexican contingency of his business is still operating as usual. I haven't been here in years, but everything is exactly the same, a testament to my father's high standards.

My mobile phone rings. It's my father's defense attorney, Jefferson Whitley.

"Mr. Whitley," I answer.

"Mr. Estrada. Is now a good time to talk?"

"It is."

"Good. I just wanted to update you on a few things. I have good news and bad news. The good news is, I may be able to get your father released until trial. We're asking for a reduced bail amount, and the hearing is scheduled for next week. The bad news is, you're still going to have to come up with at least half a million to make that happen."

"It's not a problem," I respond. We have millions of dollars in a clean bank account if we need it.

"Good, then I'll keep you posted. I think it's best if you steer clear of the hearing."

"Yes, sir." I'm not sure if I'm more stressed or relieved that my father will be out of prison soon.

The phone clicks, and he's gone. I'm sure that call will cost me two hundred and fifty dollars. I grumble under my breath as I take a moment to check for other messages and texts. My finger hovers over Emilia's name. I just want to hear her voice, to see if she'll speak with me, but then the front door swings open and Rogelio enters with another man.

"Alejandro. This is Fernando. You two have never met. He's taking over for me out front for the evening. I'll be back in the morning."

I shake Fernando's hand.

"Let me know if you need anything," Fernando responds before closing the door.

I spend some time reacquainting myself with the ranch. I haven't been here since I was a kid. After my mom died, I never came to Mexico. We used to vacation at this house while my dad was here for business. I have such bittersweet memories of this house and being here as a family when I was young.

The doors to my dad's office are open, and I step inside. A large, hand-carved wooden desk takes up the center of the room. A laptop sits on the desk with its screen closed, and bookshelves line an entire wall. Dispersed amongst books are small, decorative items and a few framed pictures. One large frame holds a picture of my mom. Her long, dark hair is swept back over her shoulders, her head tipped back in laughter, and her hand over her heart. A smile tugs at my lips at the pure joy emanating from her face, but that smile quickly disappears as I remember that it was this business that took her from me—from my family. If I really think about it, this business that has given our family its wealth and reputation has also taken everything. My mother is dead, my father in jail, our family torn apart. I have nothing. Except…

Emilia…

I sit down at the desk, open the laptop, and enter the password that pulls up contact names, addresses, business information, and financials. Long ago, my father and I agreed on a password in the event that one of us would be incapacitated. Another reality of this life.

The screen comes to life and folders populate the screen. I spend the next hour doing spreadsheets, moving money in and out of bank accounts, and sending out emails. While the goods we're moving are illegal, we operate like a legitimate business. And as I sit here, I feel much more at home. This is where I belong, behind the desk, not running shipments of heroin, weed, guns, and setting up transportation routes for smuggling people into the country. I run the business. I have no business wielding a gun and running drugs.

An hour later, and I'm still scrolling through endless files, saving the ones I don't have at home to a flash drive. There's a light knock on the door, and a young woman peeks her head inside.

"Mr. Estrada. I'm Esperanza, your father's housekeeper. May I bring you anything to eat or drink?" She looks barely eighteen, her hair pulled into a ponytail and her dark brown eyes doe-eyed and innocent. I hate when my father hires young girls. I hope her involvement here doesn't get her killed.

I shake my head. "No thank you."

"I'll have breakfast ready for you in the morning. If you need anything, I'll be in the back house." She closes the door, and it's then that I remember a small living quarter behind the house.

I spin in my father's office chair and open French doors that look out onto the spacious back yard. A large pool spans the majority of the yard, surrounded by lush landscaping and lights. You'd never know this little oasis was inside a compound on the edge of a poor, desolate Mexican town.

Through the pool lights and the glow of the landscaping lights, I barely make out the small stucco house, Esperanza's quarters. It must've been recently built, as it looks like a fairly new structure. Also, it wasn't there when I was a child. The pool has been refinished and expanded. It used to be a small circle in the ground. My mom and brother and I would play for hours in the water, the humid air and scorching sun never deterring us. I smile as I glance toward the corner of the patio where my mom would always lie in a lounge chair, watching us boys roughhouse in the water.

Swallowing hard, I step outside and sit down on one of the plush lounge chairs scattered around the perimeter of the pool. I lace my fingers behind my head and lie back to stare at the dark sky full of stars. Even with a few scattered clouds, the moon is bright and the sky is clear. A far cry from the brown, smog-covered skies of Phoenix. Many things are so different from Phoenix—it's a slower pace of life here. I appreciate the relaxed nature of Mexico. I wonder what Emilia's doing right now. As twisted as it sounds, I almost wish she was packing her bags and leaving. She deserves better than this—better than me.

As much as I try to relish in the good memories of this house, of Mexico, I can't. I'm unsettled here. This house is where the business began, the business that stole my mother and tore my family apart. The evil started here.

A light flickers in Esperanza's quarters, illuminating the windows. The side of the house facing the pool is a sliding glass door and there are no window coverings. From here, I can see it's a studio set-up; to the right is a full-sized bed, a small nightstand, and three-drawer chest. To the left is a small door that leads to a bathroom, and there's a small kitchen. A loveseat and bookshelf complete the place, and the walls are bare, only a few personal belongings on top of the chest of drawers.

I know I should move, give the girl her privacy, but seeing her reminds me of Emilia.

Esperanza unbuttons her uniform dress, and it slides down her body to the floor. She wears nothing under her dress and her tan skin is on full display. Her breasts hang heavy, and a shock of dark hair stands out between her legs. She lies nude on the loveseat and rests her head on the armrest. Watching her does nothing for me. Emilia is the only woman who has an effect on me. Emilia. God, I miss her.

I hear the latch on the side gate click, and I immediately reach for my gun, which is tucked behind me. I sit still, waiting, listening to the rocks crunch under heavy footsteps as they draw closer. A dark form moves behind the shrubbery and heads toward Esperanza's door, coming into view. Rogelio.

Blowing out a silent breath, I push myself up and decide to call it a night. I have no desire to see Rogelio and Esperanza get each other off. I lock the patio doors behind me and find my way to the spare bedroom where I'll stay. Decorated in traditional Mexican flair, the hand carved furniture sits prominently in the room. Exhausted, I lie down on the bed and close my eyes, but not before checking my phone to see if Emilia has reached out.

Negative.

Sleep hasn't come easily these last few months, and tonight is no different. In between bouts of restlessness, I find rare minutes of sleep. But those moments come apart in a burst of gunfire and screaming. I yank my gun from the nightstand and throw open the closet door. My dad keeps weapons in every closet, every drawer, and in hidden compartments behind pictures throughout the house. I lift the rifle from its hook and fling the bedroom door open, sticking close to the wall, the rifle butting into my arm. If someone aims at me, I'll fucking shoot them.

I hear multiple voices, male, shouting near the front of the house, and the front door wide fucking open. When I see that the men yelling are all mine, I relax and approach. Rogelio and Fernando are spewing at each other in Spanish, and while I understand what they're saying, I tell them to shut up in English. Everyone stills, and all eyes turn to me.

Rogelio runs his hand through his hair and glances at the ground, looking angry and somewhat ashamed. A man lies on the ground in a pool of blood.

"What the fuck happened?" I yell.

"He jumped the wall. We shot."

"Jesus Christ." I rake my hands up and down my face. I've seen more blood in the last three days than I've seen in the last three years. "Who is it?"

"Not sure. No ID."

I come closer, studying the dead man, but step back quickly to avoid stepping in the blood that has pooled around him. "Is he armed?"

"Negative," Rogelio says, teeth gritted.

"Fuck. It's probably some kid…" My voice trails off. *Shit,*

shit. Some innocent kid got shot on my family property simply because of this fucking business…

"Boss. Orders are if anyone comes over that wall or through that gate uninvited… Shoot." Rogelio stands stiffly.

A muscle moves in my jaw. "Whose orders?"

"Your father's."

"And where is he?" I bark at the men.

"In the States," Rogelio sneers.

"Where in the motherfucking States?" I'm about to fucking lose it. I can't stand this anymore.

"Arizona."

"Don't fucking get smart with me. His ass is in a federal prison," I seethe. "I'm running the show, and my orders are do not fucking shoot anyone until we've identified them as a threat. Do you understand?"

Rogelio narrows his eyes, clearly agitated with me. He gestures toward Fernando to follow him and begins walking away.

"And, Rogelio." I glare at him. "No fucking the staff."

He blinks in shock that I would know, but he nods briskly. "I'll take care of this." Rogelio kicks the foot of the dead man at our feet, and I turn around, heading back inside.

Esperanza is in the kitchen, wringing her hands together. "Is everything okay?" she asks in a hushed voice.

"Yes." Obviously, that's a lie. I'm standing in the hallway with a fucking rifle and a handgun, and there's a dead man on the front lawn.

"I'll have breakfast ready in a few minutes. I didn't expect you up this early." Her voice is timid and shaky.

Her demeanor would normally soften me if it weren't for how out of it I am. "I didn't plan to be up this early. I'm going to shower; no hurry on the food."

She smiles at me as I walk away. Securing the rifle back in the closet, I bring my handgun with me to the bathroom, hiding it under a hand towel on the counter. Turning on the shower, I strip and leave my clothes in a pile on the floor. As steam fills the bathroom, I catch a glimpse of myself in the mirror. I stare and I stare at that man. I barely recognize him anymore. I'm disgusted, ashamed. Who am I?

Stepping into the hot shower, I let the water burn my skin just so I'll feel something—anything. The scalding water reminds me of Emilia. Her gaze, her touch, her presence burns me in a way I've never felt.

It makes me *feel*.

She makes me feel.

Everything about her burns through the evil exterior of who I really am, and she sees the good in me. She gives me hope at a life outside of this, even though I know the reality—there is no hope. She's selfless and sweet and everything I've ever desired.

I punch the tile wall in frustration, gasping at the pain in my hand, even though the pain in me hurts more. This fucking world I live in has taken everything important from me.

My past, my present, and any hope for a future.

chapter twelve

Emilia

ALEX HAS BEEN gone for four days. I know this because I've counted every hour he's been gone. I've worked every day, hoping that time will pass faster, only it doesn't. Each day, I come home and Rosa is here, cooking for me and trying to distract me, but it doesn't work. This morning, as I lie in his bed, I send him a text. Three words.

"I miss you."

I get nothing in return.

I SLAM THE metal door on the coffee machine and press the start button before moving on to the next drip machine and repeating the process. Jax eyes me carefully, not approaching me. Obviously, my mood speaks to how I'm feeling this morning. He slowly scrawls the daily coffee special and a meaningful quote on the chalkboard. I love his quotes. I find myself looking forward to them every morning.

Today, however, I just don't care.

Megan took the day off. She let us know yesterday that she's so pleased with how well and efficiently we work together that she was leaving the shop to us today. It's Friday, the busiest day of the week, but Jax and I assured her we could handle it. I need the busyness to keep my mind distracted anyway.

I stock the display case with pastries and muffins and prep the creamer, milk, and sugar station.

"Talk to me, sunshine," Jax says sympathetically as he leans back against the counter. His legs are crossed in front of him and his arms are folded over his chest.

I sigh deeply and mimic his position on the counter behind me so we're facing each other. "Just life."

"Ah, come on. It's more than that. You're the most positive person I've ever met, Em. What's got you all moody this morning? You haven't been yourself for a couple of days."

I shrug. "Just a lot on my mind." *To say the least.*

He nods and twists his lips for a moment. "So, uh, I know we spend every day together, but do you, uh, want to go to a concert tonight? It's a local band that one of my buddies plays in. They have a gig at a bar in Uptown Phoenix. Just friends." He holds his hands up innocently. "Sounds like the cure for your mood. Music and shitty beer."

I laugh at him, although the invitation sounds great. "That actually sounds really fun, but I'm going to have to pass. Can we do it another time?"

He frowns but doesn't push it. "Yeah, they play pretty much every weekend. But I'm holding you to it. You need to get out, meet people, have a good time."

He's right, of course. Since I've come here, I've only met a handful of people. "I know, and I will. I promise." I scold myself for being a homebody. I shouldn't be waiting around for Alex.

He flings a towel at me, and I catch it before it hits me in the face. He laughs and walks around the counter to unlock the front door and get this day started. It's insanely busy today. So much so that Jax and I barely say two words to each other that aren't about making more coffee, refilling creamer, restocking pastries, or wiping down tables. It's actually nice not worrying about checking my phone every hour on the hour.

When I look at the clock again, it's two thirty and the next shift comes on at three. I'm wiping down tables while Jax finishes filling out paperwork from our shift and getting the day's deposit ready, when the front door swings open.

It's Sam. I haven't seen him in the last two days, but he's crossed my mind many times.

"Hey, stranger," he says with a smile.

"Hey." I'm surprised at how excited I sound.

"How've you been?"

"Good," I lie. *Because I've been shit. Total shit. And lonely.* I wring the washcloth in my hands. There's something familiar about the way Sam watches me, but I can't put my finger on it. My stomach does a little dip.

"Can I take you to dinner tonight?" he asks. He's direct. I like that about him.

"Ummm." I wipe my sweaty palms on my hips and shift on my feet. In my periphery, Jax clears his throat loudly, but keeps his gaze on the paperwork. The silence is awkward, and I can see a hint of frustration on Sam's face. He breaks up the silence by

174

calling out to Jax.

"Hey, Jax." I stall for time. "Can you get me a medium dark roast? Leave a little room," Sam asks.

"You got it," Jax says, dropping the paperwork on the counter and pulling a cardboard cup down from the shelf.

Sam walks away and takes a seat at a table, and I glance out the window at Andres, wondering how I'll ever be able to shake him for the evening if I accept Sam's invitation. I stay near the counter and fight with myself on whether I should go to dinner with him.

Jax sets Sam's coffee in front of me. "Sunshine. Take the man up on it. It's dinner." He encourages me with his eyes, and I sigh.

Sam watches me intently as I walk his coffee over to him. He raises his eyebrows as I approach. "Coffee delivery. Nice," he says as I set the hot coffee in front of him. His eyes go from humorous to sincere in one second as he asks me again, "Have dinner with me, Emilia. I've enjoyed talking to you, and I'd like to get to know you better."

Heat crawls across my chest, and I scratch nervously at my neck. "I like talking to you too," I admit. I feel like I'm betraying Alex by even considering this.

"Here." He pulls out a piece of paper with his phone number scribbled on it. "My cell number is on there. It's *just* dinner, Emilia." He smirks at me. "Call or text when you get off work and let me know." His lips pull into a full smile and his eyes beg me to say yes. "And I know you're off work in the next half hour, so I expect an answer fairly soon."

I chew nervously on my bottom lip. "Okay, I'll let you know."

He stands up and pulls a ten-dollar bill from his wallet. "For the coffee."

"No. I've got this," I stammer.

He rolls his eyes good-naturedly. "Just take the money, Emilia."

I shove his hand away as he laughs playfully, waving to get Jax's attention. "Jax, your girl won't take my money. She says it's no good here."

"Sunshine, take the man's money," Jax grumbles, shaking his head at us and our banter.

"I've gotta go. Talk to you soon, Emilia." He slaps the ten on the counter on his way out.

Jax sighs, annoyed. "Sunshine, that man is into you."

"No, he's not." I flush, embarrassed.

As Jax and I wrap up our shift and I'm hanging up my apron, Jax shuffles over and hands me another envelope with today's tips. I shove it into my back pocket.

"Go to dinner with the man, sunshine. Put him out of his misery. Oh, and I want details on Monday." I struggle for a moment, but I decide that dinner with a friend might be good for me.

"Deal."

"HI, ROSA!" I announce as I burst through the front door, suddenly excited for my dinner date tonight.

"Hi, *mija*." She looks up from her cookbook.

"What're you making?" I set my wallet and phone on the

kitchen counter.

"Not sure yet. Looking for something to make you for dinner."

"Oh, don't worry about me." I wave a hand at her. "I picked up an extra shift at the coffee shop tonight, so I won't be around for dinner." I feel terrible lying, but I can't really tell her I'm going on a date either. "But maybe, tomorrow night, you could make me homemade macaroni and cheese?" I love that Rosa enjoys cooking, it's a nice change of pace for me, after having to always prepare meals for the last ten years.

"That I can do." She slams the cookbook closed. "Mr. Estrada had strict orders to make sure I feed you. Are you sure you'll be okay without dinner tonight?"

"I will. I'll grab a sandwich at work."

Rosa shoves the cookbook back in the cupboard and pulls off her apron. Her dark hair is in a ponytail and her caramel skin is flawless with no make-up.

"Rosa, have you heard from him?"

She stills. Her back is facing me. "I haven't."

That's what I thought. "I'm worried about him. He hasn't called or returned any of my text messages."

"I know you are," she says sympathetically.

"He's been gone all week, and I haven't heard a word." Unease settles into the pit of my stomach. I love Alex, but I'm angry that he could so easily pack up and leave for another country and not bother once to check in. I realize that maybe these feelings are unfounded. He said it himself. He couldn't give me *more*, but I know he feels what I'm feeling. I can see it in his eyes and in his actions. But now, I'm not so sure. He left me and went to Mexico without so much as a goodbye.

I should probably feel guilty about going out with Sam, but I don't. Sam feels safe to me, where Alex now feels reckless. I'm in love with Alex, but at what cost? Could I live with him vanishing to foreign countries and never checking in? I exhale loudly in frustration.

Rosa turns around and begins folding her apron before slipping it into a kitchen drawer. "It's how it has to be, Emilia. Remember what I told you the other day. The less you know, the better."

"I don't want to know anything other than that he's okay."

"I know, sweetheart. If I hear from Mr. Estrada, I will let you know." She offers me a sympathetic smile and places her hand on mine as she walks around me. "Well then, I'll get here early tomorrow and make sure you have a nice breakfast."

"No need to get here early," I rush to say. Not sure how late I'll be tonight. "I plan to sleep in tomorrow. It's been a long week. I'll see you in the morning."

I grab my phone and head into my bathroom to run a warm bath. I dump bubble bath into the water and twist my hair into a bun, then send a quick text message to Sam, agreeing to meet him for dinner. He responds almost immediately with the name of a Mexican restaurant, and I tell him I'll meet him there. I spend the next half hour soaking in the warm, lilac-scented water, scheming up a plan to lose Andres—which is looking like it could be a chore in and of itself.

After my bath, I spend an ungodly amount of time getting ready for dinner. I change into a floral print shift dress and curl my hair so that it hangs long and wavy. I touch up my makeup and slip my feet into a pair of wedge sandals.

The condo is silent, but I know I'm being watched,

evidenced by the security cameras all over the place. I try not to look suspicious, so I keep my normal routine, stopping by the refrigerator for a bottle of water, playing around on my phone, then slipping out the front door. I shake my head when I think that Alex probably knows my every move and that's why he hasn't called or responded to my text. Between the security cameras and Andres, he has to know every move I make. It angers me that he's not considerate enough to address my concern for him in return.

The downtown streets are emptying out for the evening, and it's not long before I sense Andres nearby. I don't bother to look over my shoulder anymore—I know he's there. I follow the same path I always do to Café Au Lait. Pulling open the front door, I step into the dimly lit café. It looks so different in the evening; peaceful, actually. The lights are turned down, the music is less upbeat, more calming. The place is full of students studying and people on their laptops.

I see Holly behind the counter with her bright red hair and porcelain skin. We met briefly yesterday as I was leaving and she was coming in. "Hi, Holly," I greet her.

She smiles widely. "Hi, Emilia. What brings you here?"

"I think I left my cell here this afternoon. Have you seen it?" I feel bad lying to Holly, but I need to create a distraction so I can lose Andres.

"I haven't. You might want to check Megan's office. If Jax found it, he may have put it on her desk." She nods to the closed door of the backroom that doubles as Megan's office. A couple people line up at the counter, and I set my wallet down to help her, still stalling for time.

"Here." I step out of the way. "I'll ring them up, you make

coffee." I smile at her. I ring up the two customers and glance out the front window, finding Andres in his normal position. Perfect.

"You're all set," I tell her when the line has dwindled. "I'm just going to check the back for my phone, and I'll let myself out the back door."

"Sounds good. Thanks for the help, Emilia."

I give her a goodbye wave and step into the dark office. Flipping on the lights, I close the door behind me, and push open the alley door. A blast of heat hits me in the face and I squint against my dry eyes. If I go right, I'll end up on the main street again where Andres will see me. Going left will take me a couple blocks over without being noticed. I follow the map on my phone and find I'm six blocks away from the Mexican restaurant where I'm meeting Sam.

Two wooden doors adorn the entrance. They appear to be hand carved and heavy, with large, iron hinges holding them in place. How quaint. I wait for Sam outside the entrance on an intricate bench that matches the doors. Clouds are building out east, much like they have all week, and they look like large cotton balls in the sky. There is a slight breeze, and the hot, dry air stings my nostrils.

"Have you been waiting long?" Sam's deep voice pulls me away from my daydreaming.

"No. I just got here." I stand up to meet him.

He pulls me into a short hug and kisses my cheek. "Let's go inside. I've got reservations for us at seven." He holds the door open for me, ever the gentleman. Inside, a hostess meets us and recognizes Sam, her eyes widening a bit at the sight of me next to him.

"Mr. Cortez." She smiles warmly at him.

"Savannah," he acknowledges her.

"Your table is ready." She guides us to a small table in the back. The glow of a candle centerpiece creates a wonderful ambience. Its iron base is twisted into the same design as the door handles I noticed earlier. Someone designed this place impeccably.

Sam pulls out the chair for me, and our server immediately descends upon the table with a basket of chips and a small clover-shaped dish with different sauces. Sam orders us sparkling water and pomegranate margaritas.

"I hope you like Mexican food. Those are different flavors of salsa." He smiles at me and points to the clover-shaped dish.

"I've never really had it. Wait, I take that back." I tap my chin. "On the bus ride to Arizona, we stopped at a Taco Bell. Their nachos are amazing."

"Taco Bell," he scoffs. "That's not Mexican food. And nachos? You mean processed cheese drizzled on stale chips? If you want to taste some amazing nachos, I'll order you some nachos."

I light up at the idea, setting my menu aside. "Nachos would be great."

"I'll tell you what. I'm going to order a bunch of stuff, but…" His eyes glimmer with amusement. "You have to try it all." My eyes must widen in horror, and he amends, "Just a bite. I swear this is the best Mexican food outside of Mexico itself."

Mexico. Instantly, I'm thinking about Alex, wondering about him, worrying. Again. I wonder what he's doing. *If he's safe.* When he'll be back. My stomach tightens with worry about him, but I shove those thoughts aside when the server brings us our drinks.

"Tell me what you think of the pomegranate margarita." He licks some of the salt off his glass with his tongue, and, to my surprise, heat pools in my belly when I watch him.

My heart stammers, but then I feel guilty. I'm sleeping with Alex, I'm in love with Alex, and yet I can't take my eyes off the gorgeous man across from me. I mimic him and swipe some of the salt from the rim of my own glass, sipping on the sweet drink. The saltiness mixed with the sweetness and the slight after-burn from the tequila, make for a dangerous combination.

"Oh my god, this is amazing." I take another drink.

"Slow down there, tiger." He chuckles. "These are strong, and as much as I'd love to see you tipsy, I don't intend on getting you drunk on our first date." First date. Those words cause my stomach to flip.

"Huh, a date." I laugh nervously. "Is that what this is? I thought it was just dinner," I joke with him. I know it's a date.

"It is. It's a dinner date."

He's quick with his comebacks. I like that. I blush a little as I say, "And you said 'first date,' as if you're implying there will be more than one?"

Sam takes a long pull of his margarita before setting it down. "Oh, there'll be more than one, Emilia." He's confident, but not arrogant. I find myself very attracted to that. There's something about him that reminds me of Alex; they're both dominant and controlling.

A shiver runs up my spine, and I shake my head slowly. "We'll see about that."

He busts out laughing. "This is exactly why I'm attracted to you. You're beautiful, and I can tell you're smart. But most importantly, you don't put up with anybody's shit." I've been putting up with Alex's, I think to myself. I've become weak to Alex.

"You mean your shit," I correct him, and we both laugh.

My phone starts ringing on the table and Alex's name flashes across the screen. *Holy shit!* He's finally calling me. My heart is in my throat, and I'm desperate to answer it, but I can't do that in front of Sam—for many reasons.

Sam starts to frown at me, probably because I suddenly look like I want to run. Almost in a panic, I reach over and silence my phone just as a text comes in, also from Alex. I glance at the screen before pulling it under the table to read it.

Where are you?

I also now realize that it's been an hour since I walked into Café Au Lait and snuck out the back door. Andres must've caught on that I'm no longer there. I decide it's best to respond to Alex quickly.

Out.

I power down my phone and set it back on the table. I should be ecstatic to hear from Alex. To know he's alive, but I'm more upset that it took me skirting Andres for him to reach out to me. I want badly to yell at Alex right now, but I shove those feelings aside and bring myself back to the present and Sam.

Sam's watching me intently in between sips of his margarita. "Everything okay?" he asks, cracking a tortilla chip in half and dipping it into some salsa.

"Yes." I smile nervously at him.

He doesn't believe me, but he doesn't say anything.

"What?" I ask shyly.

"I'm glad you came to dinner with me."

"Me too." It's a half lie. I'm enjoying dinner, but undeniably, I miss Alex. I swallow hard and shift uncomfortably in my chair, tucking my hair behind my ear. I try to push the guilt aside by reminding myself over and over: *it's just dinner.*

"So," he says, perking up. "Tell me why you moved here from Illinois." He shoves the small bowl of salsa and basket of chips closer to me.

"Came looking for my dad," I say after dipping a chip in salsa.

"Did you find him?"

I nod, stuffing the chip in my mouth. "I did. However, it didn't go as well as I hoped." Technically, it didn't *go* at all. He said hi, then bye, and I was gone. I waver between hurt and angry when I think about my father.

He sets his margarita on the table and leans forward, attentive. "What happened?"

I think about it for a moment, wondering if I should share it with him. If it would matter. Finally, I decide I don't really mind. It is what it is. "Honestly, he blew me off. He bailed on my mom when she found out she was pregnant. I shouldn't have been surprised that I'd be less than welcome now, being an adult, but I didn't expect outright denial. He literally told me to go away and he shut the door." I'm more confident telling Sam this story. Maybe it's the margaritas, or maybe I've suddenly come to terms with the fact that I'm alone in this world.

"I'm sorry," he says quietly, placing his hand on mine.

I pull my hand away, cringing. "Sorry I'm so depressing."

"You're not depressing, Emilia. Your dad's an asshole," he says point blank. "Any father would be blessed to have you as a daughter."

I feel a blush creeping up my face. It's a sweet thing to say. Whether it's true or not, I don't know. "So, now, I'm just working to save up some money until I figure out what I'm going to do."

"Will you stay in Phoenix?"

"I'm not sure. I never envisioned staying here without my dad."

Sam nods and rubs his chin. "What about your mom?"

"Even more depressing than my dad," I say quietly, feeling emotional just thinking about it. My mom would have loved a restaurant like this.

"Jesus, Em." He shakes his head slowly.

"We can save that story for another time." I offer a tight smile. "Tell me about you." *Please, because I don't want to talk about me anymore.*

"You're looking at it." He smiles, sitting back in his chair. "Work has pretty much consumed my life for the last five years. I graduated from college and took a job and have been working ever since. Just spent my time climbing the ranks and it left me little time for much else."

"What do you do for the government?"

"A little of this, a little of that. They keep me busy." Why is he evading my question? Maybe he's embarrassed of his job.

I sip on my delicious margarita. I'll have to see if Rosa can make something like this sometime.

"So, you don't have a girlfriend?" Yeah, that boldness was definitely the margarita.

He turns his head and chokes out a laugh. "Ah, no, Emilia. If I had a girlfriend, I wouldn't be at dinner with you."

Oh, right. "I like that answer." I laugh and dip a chip in some salsa. His eyes lock on mine for a brief moment before I drop mine and look at my margarita.

"I like you, Emilia. I'd love to get to know you better."

Before I have time to respond, our server shows up and

delivers small plates of tacos, enchiladas, tamales, rolled tacos, and another round of margaritas. In between bites of tacos and tamales, Sam and I enjoy getting to know each other. Surprisingly, we have a lot in common. By the end of dinner, our stomachs are full and we've made plans to take a desert hike once it begins to cool down for the fall.

Although my stomach turns when I think about Alex as I make plans with Sam.

"I bet you've never been on a date where a girl has eaten this much," I joke with him as I push myself away from the table. "I'm sold on Mexican food."

He laughs heartily. "I'm just glad you enjoyed dinner."

"I did. I'll definitely be coming back here."

"Let me know if you do. I'll call and let them know you're on your way."

I scrunch my eyebrows together, confused by his comment.

He explains, "My aunt and uncle own this restaurant. And another out in the East Valley. My uncle was born and raised here in Phoenix, but has family in Mexico. He spent a lot of time there growing up. All of these decorations were imported from Mexico." He waves his hand around the room that is decorated in Mexican style décor, including mirrors, wrought-iron chandeliers, and paintings.

My eyebrows shoot up. "Your family owns this place?" I'm seriously impressed. My body warms as the tequila from the margaritas I've been drinking finally settles in.

"They do. I used to work here growing up. I bussed tables all through high school." He says it with pride, which makes me like him even more. The guy respects hard work. That's a great quality.

"Well, please tell them that, for someone who's never had Mexican food aside from Taco Bell, I'm pretty sure theirs is the best."

"I'll pass that message along. With Taco Bell as their competitor," he teases, "I'm sure they'll be glad to know they've ranked first on your list." He gets up and pulls out my chair, then reaches out to help me stand, but never releases my hand. Instead, he repositions it as we walk toward the exit.

He waves goodbye to some of the staff and holds the door for me again as we step outside. The wind has picked up, and lightning is shooting across the sky.

"Storm's rolling in," he says. "We haven't had a good one in a few weeks. I love the summer monsoons."

"Then I'm going to get going. I have a few blocks to walk and want to beat the rain."

He looks at me like I'm ridiculous. "You're not walking."

"It's not that far. I'm just a few blocks that way." I point in the general direction of the tall office buildings.

He shakes his head, adamant. "I'm driving you home, Em. Get your ass in the car." He pushes the button on his key fob and the headlights flash on a black Mercedes in the next row over.

"I'll be fine," I insist. "I'll text you when I get home."

"Get in the car, Emilia." He all but drags me to his car by my elbow as I concede. I'm glad he insisted on driving me as large raindrops begin to bounce off the windshield not more than a minute later. He opens the front door, and I slide into the warm leather seats; then he gets in on his side. A flash of panic spreads through me as I wonder if Andres will be waiting for me.

He pushes a button on his dash and the car purrs to life. "Where to?"

"Um, right by Café Au Lait. I'm just a couple blocks down from there." I power up my phone while Sam weaves through the downtown streets, and we get closer to Café Au Lait. My phone begins to chime with text messages, but I shove it down into my purse. "That brown brick building on the corner. Just stop here, I'll walk across the street."

"That's where you live?" Sam's voice is filled with surprise.

"Well, my roommate owns the place. I just have a room." I hate saying "roommate," but at this point, I don't know what we are.

He shoots a concerned glance at me. "Let me park and I'll walk you up. I don't want you walking alone."

I almost groan. I don't need another man thinking I can't take care of myself. It's Phoenix, not Detroit. "I'll be fine," I blurt out. "But thank you for dinner. I really had a lot of fun."

He grips the steering wheel and stares at the building before turning to me. "So did I." Then he leans over and presses a gentle kiss to my cheek. Tiny butterflies fly around in my belly. "Goodnight, Emilia."

"Night, Sam." A smile tugs at my lips as I run my fingers over the spot on my cheek where Sam kissed me. I can't deny an attraction to him. He's a lot like Alex, only different. Where Alex is dangerous, Sam is professional. Both are remarkably attractive.

I jog through the lobby and take the elevator to the top floor. Exiting, I scan the area for any sign of Andres. All clear. Inside, lights from the kitchen illuminate the hallway, and I exhale, my heart rate returning to normal. I did it. I made it back without suspicion. But in the living room, I stop suddenly when I see a dark figure on the couch.

It's Andres, his face contorted in anger. Standing, he pulls his cell from his jacket and presses a button. I can see the veins in his forehead pulsing. This is not good.

"She's here." That's all that's said before he deposits the phone back into the pocket of his jacket. I move to pass him, but he steps into my way, tall and bulky.

"Excuse me," I say, trying to move around him again.

This time, he steps aside, but not before grabbing me by the arm. "What you did tonight will never happen again. Do you understand me?" His grip is firm.

A pained cry falls from my lips. Yanking my arm out of his grasp, I narrow my eyes at him and turn away, walking down the hall to Alex's room.

"Answer me, Emilia." His voice is low and raspy and scares me.

I don't want to answer him. He's Alex's dog. I don't deserve to be treated this way, and he doesn't deserve my answer. Because my life is none of his damn business. It's my life. I appreciate Alex's attentiveness to my safety and his willingness to protect me, but I will not be bullied by a bodyguard.

Even though I spent the evening with Sam, I can only think about Alex. I retreat to the only room in this house that I feel safe. Even when he's gone, I feel Alex here. Kicking off my shoes, I pull my dress off over my head. There's a white, ribbed tank-style undershirt of Alex's lying folded on the floor, and I unfasten my bra, tossing it to the ground before pulling on the shirt. Pulling back the covers on Alex's bed, I slide into the middle and place pillows all around me. I'm cocooned in his scent, but there's nothing that'll replace the feel of his arms wrapped tightly around me. I miss him.

chapter thirteen
Alex

AGITATION AND WORRY run through me, and I feel myself slowly losing control. I'm exhausted as I pace the Saltillo-tiled floor in my father's office, waiting for Andres to call me back. He's the best guy I have. He doesn't lose people—but he lost Emilia.

The phone rings and I answer without pleasantries. "Anything yet?"

"No," Andres says calmly. Motherfucking calm.

Rage roils through me, and Andres is calm. I slam the phone on the desk and run my fingers through my hair. "Goddammit, Emilia!" I wish she was standing in front of me so I could give her a verbal beating. One word, one fucking word she texted to me. *Out.* Like that was a fucking explanation.

I've never been angrier.

I tried tracking her phone, but with it powered down, I was unable to locate her. I called Café Au Lait. They said she stopped in to look for her phone and left. This is where Andres claims he lost her. The old-fashioned grandfather clock on the wall thrums nine times. Nine o'clock. I have to make a quick decision. Leave tonight or tomorrow. If I leave tonight, the border closes in two hours, and I'm an hour and a half away.

I pull my bag from the closet and begin yanking open drawers to remove clothes. I shove them into the bag haphazardly and lock up the house. Tossing the duffle bag into the backseat of my car, I pull up to the gate and Rogelio opens it. A confused look crosses his face.

"I need to head back to the States. Got a few things to take care of. Will you be okay handling things around here?"

"Yeah." He nods. "Everything okay?"

"Don't know."

"I've got Mexico under control." He smirks. I want to fucking punch that smirk off his face.

"No more messes, Rogelio." There has been enough blood on my hands, and I'm done. Done with all of it.

"Yes, sir. Drive careful. I'll have Juan Santiago follow you into Sonoyta to make sure you get to the border without any problems."

I nod at him and pull through the gates. My car idles as I impatiently tap my thumb on the steering wheel until I see the old beater pick-up truck pull up behind me. Then I punch the gas and take off for the border under the dark Mexican sky, leaving a trail of dust and hard decisions behind me.

The roads are single lane and wind through small mountains and plains, the only light coming from my headlights. I pass only a handful of cars. Most people stay locked inside at night, away from the monsters destroying this country—monsters like me. Miles ahead, I see the flickering lights of Sonoyta. Twenty minutes later, I'm rolling into town, following the signs that lead me to the

U.S. border. Juan Santiago flashes his headlights behind me as he turns off onto a side street, and I sit in the one lane open for entry into the United States.

Along the dirt trail beside me, a frail lady peddles homemade tortillas, hoping for cash, and taco stands line the street. I pull into the bay where I hand a U.S. border official my passport. He eyes me skeptically, looking over my shoulder into the backseat of my SUV, before sending me off to secondary inspection.

"Fuck!" I yell and smack the steering wheel. I'm not concerned they'll find anything because they won't. I left all the guns and drugs in Mexico, but it's my time that's valuable—my time getting back to Emilia. I'm angry with her for ditching Andres, but mostly, I'm worried about her. I pull into the secondary inspection bay and kill the engine, following the agent into a small holding room.

An hour crawls by. *A fucking hour.* I've never considered how seconds feel like hours until something you love is missing. I love Emilia. I admit it. I pinch my eyes closed and rub my temples. My cell has no reception in this room, and I tap my foot nervously on the dirty tile floor. A television blares reruns of *Family Feud*, and I rest my head back against the wall. My stomach churns as panic settles in. I envision Emilia in the hands of my enemies. A pawn in a game she's not a part of. Hurt because of me. This isn't right. She can't be hurt. She never did anything. Her being a part of my life is my own fucking fault. I knew I shouldn't have picked her up that day.

Selfish. You're a selfish bastard, you know that?

Yes, I know. Loud and fucking clear.

And I know I don't deserve to, but I pray. I pray harder than I've ever prayed before. I confess my sins, and I make promises I don't know if I'll be able to keep, but swear I'll try as long as Emilia is safe.

"Mr. Estrada," the husky voice growls at me. I sit up quickly. "You're all set to go." He holds my passport in his hand. I take it as I pass him, and he escorts me back to my vehicle. Clothes are strewn about the back seat, and everything from inside the glove box and center console is scattered everywhere. Normally, I'd be fucking pissed, but I just need to get back to Phoenix and find Emilia. That's all I care about—Emilia.

As I pull out of the border patrol station and onto the dark single lane, my phone rings. It's Andres. When I press the answer button on my steering wheel, his voice comes through the speakers. "She's here." A click on the other end of the line indicates he's hung up before I can respond.

And now my worry is replaced with anger as I step on the gas.

ANDRES LEANS AGAINST the counter in my kitchen, sipping on a mug of hot coffee. He looks as angry as I feel. I toss my keys on the counter and slide into a chair. Andres takes a seat next to me and sets his mug on the table.

"So, what the hell happened?" I ask him.

He looks me in the eye and shakes his head slightly. "Don't know. She ditched me. In all my years doing security, I've never lost a client. Ever."

"Did she say where she was?

"Nah. She's a young girl, Alex. She was probably dancing at a bar or having drinks and she didn't want me there." His eyes drop to his hands, which are laced together, and he cracks his knuckles

"What's wrong?"

Andres shrugs. "It's probably nothing, boss, but she's been chatting up Detective Cortez at the coffee shop."

Cortez? Fucking Cortez?

My heart races, and I see nothing but red.

"Goddammit!" I smack the table. Andres sits up straighter, shocked by my outburst. I never let my emotions show, but when it comes to Emilia, and when it comes to Cortez, I lose it. "What do you mean, chatting up?"

"He goes in for coffee every day. He flirts with her. Obviously, I'm not inside. I can't hear what's being said, but they talk for a few minutes. It looks innocent."

"Nothing is innocent with that piece of shit. How come you didn't tell me before?" I run my fingers through my hair and pinch the bridge of my nose. "Was she with him tonight?"

He shakes his head, helpless. "Don't know. Honestly."

"How many times have they talked?"

"Four, five times, maybe. Like I said, he goes in every day for coffee. They talk for a few minutes and he leaves. She doesn't look upset, and I bet he doesn't even know she's with you."

"With me," I mumble and snort. "He knows something or he would never pursue her."

"I wouldn't be so sure of that."

"He does. He's using her." I'm certain of it and I'm fucking pissed off.

"For what?" Andres frowns.

"To get to me." I can feel the dull pain of a headache forming behind my eyes. "Andres, this can't happen again. You cannot lose her."

"I understand. But *she*," he nods his head toward the hallway, "needs to understand that."

"I'll handle her." I sigh and stand up from the table. "Go ahead and take off. I'll give you a call tomorrow."

"It won't happen again, boss."

"I know it won't. Goodnight." It's an observation but also a threat. Andres understands that.

When I hear the door close, I head to Emilia's room. The door is cracked open, and I peek in. Her bed is empty, perfectly made. My stomach drops, wondering if she was able to elude Andres for a second time in one day. And my heart nearly stops as I wonder if she's gone for good. Left me, as she should. Moving down the hall, I open my bedroom door. Despite how pissed I am, I instantly relax at the sight of her curled up in a ball on my bed, a pillow pressed against her stomach. The bedside light is on, but she's sound asleep.

Her deep breaths and the slight rise and fall of her shoulders tell me she's sleeping peacefully. I watch her for a few minutes, taking in the sight of her long hair splayed on my pillow, her soft porcelain skin a contrast against the dark grey sheets. Her pink lips, slightly parted, are calling to me.

"What have you done to me?" I whisper as I watch her. The question is for me, not for her. Because I never realized how lost I was before she came to me, before I found her. And I never realized how lonely I was in Mexico until I saw her just now. She's changed me. She makes me want to be a better man. She makes me want to plan a future. Set goals. And every time I think of a future, it's her I see with me.

Her long, bare legs are bent at the knees, and her arms are

wrapped tightly around that pillow. I sit on the edge of my bed and reach out to touch her leg, but my hand stills as she rolls onto her back. Her eyes flutter open and she gasps and pulls away.

"It's me, Em," I say quietly, trying to not startle her more.

"Alex?" she whispers, bewildered.

"It's me." My heart races when she says my name.

"You're back?" She blinks as if she can't believe it.

I swallow hard and nod. "I am."

She crawls into my lap, her long legs dangling off of mine. Her head fits into the crook of my neck as she leans into me. "I'm so angry at you." Her voice breaks. "You left me."

"For business." *And I'm angry at you*, I want to tell her, but I can't seem to manage it in this moment, with her soft curves pressing into me, making me feel things I don't want to feel, think things I don't want to think.

"Why didn't you tell me you were leaving? Why didn't you call me while you were gone?"

I comb a hand through her hair. *Fuck, her hair is so soft.* "I needed to give you time to absorb what I told you about me… about my business."

She sighs. "I have a million questions, some you won't like. But, Alex, what you told me doesn't change how I feel about you."

"It should," I admit. My heart is torn—I want her to love me, but she should hate me.

"It won't. It never will." Her fingers grasp my shirt tightly, and she sniffles softly. Tears fall from her eyes and onto her bare legs. I watch a single tear travel from her thigh and roll down onto my pants. "You won't scare me away." Her voice cracks. "Just don't leave me, Alex. Don't ever leave me like that again. I was so scared."

"Em, where were you tonight?" I rub her cheek with the back of my knuckles. Her skin is so soft and perfect.

"I went to dinner with a friend from the coffee shop. That's it."

Cortez? I keep that burning thought to myself. "Why did you ditch Andres?"

"Because, Alex. I hate having someone follow me. I just want to be able to go to the store or have dinner with a friend without being followed." There's a bitter note to her voice.

"It's for your protection, Em. I've told you this. Andres is not open for negotiation."

She nods, not totally agreeing, but for now, she doesn't argue.

"Who were you with?" This is her chance to tell me the truth—to see if I can trust her. My heart stands still as I wait for her to answer me.

"His name is Sam. Sam Cortez. I met him at the coffee shop. He's just a friend, I swear."

My jaw clenches when she says his name. That fucker wants my family behind bars. He's been working for years to take me out, but more importantly, he'd do anything to hurt me.

Even taking the one thing I don't deserve—Emilia.

"What do you know about him?"

"He and his co-worker come in for coffee every day. We've talked a few times. He's really nice, Alex. We had a friendly dinner. That's all. I promise."

He's nice, she says, and I grit my teeth. I can barely stomach listening to her talk about him. "Emilia, he's been trying to take my family out for years. He wants me behind bars. He's already got my father, but he wants to destroy *me*. You have to stay away from him. He'll do anything to hurt me… even if that means hurting you."

Tears fill her eyes, but I can still see the fear in them. "He's not a good man. You need to listen to me when I tell you to stay away from him." She nods her head in agreement.

I calm slightly when I believe she's told me the truth. "Look at me." I turn her shoulders so she faces me. "This…" I swipe a tear off her cheek with my thumb. "This is what I don't want to do to you. Make you cry or have you worried or scared. But that's all I can offer. I'll make you cry. I will cause you pain." *I hate hurting you, Em. I love you.*

Her eyes search mine and I have to look away. Her chin quivers, although she does her best to keep her composure. It kills me to see her hurting.

As I hold her, I think about a lot of things. My voice is soft as I tell her, "The entire time I was in Mexico, I prayed I'd come home and find you were gone. Hoped you'd pack up your stuff and move away where you'd be safe… from me, my business. Andres even had strict orders that if you were packing, he was to let you go."

She's silent for a moment, then, "I don't want to go. I want you, Alex."

Those words break my resolve.

I pull her pink lips to mine; warm, soft, and salty from her tears. Tears that I'm to blame for. I deepen our kiss and she inhales sharply.

"I need you," she mumbles against my lips.

Those three words hold so much meaning—she needs me now, but she needs me to be the man she deserves. She shifts on my lap, wrapping her legs around my waist. Her soft breasts press against my chest, and I can hear her breathing hitch as my hands grip her sides.

She's sexy as fuck in my white ribbed tank top—a tank top she won't be wearing for long. My fingers tease the soft skin just under the hem before I push the tank top over her head and toss it to the floor.

She presses her forehead to mine, her finger rubbing slow circles at the base of my neck. "Make love to me, Alex," she whispers, the words almost inaudible. "Love me."

And I will.

There is nowhere in the world I'd rather be than buried deep within her. All of her. Her body. Her heart. Her soul. She is the good I seek. She is the pure I long to be. She is worth everything I will give up to be with her.

She slides off of me and pulls off her panties, kicking them aside. She's naked in front of me, her long hair wavy and unruly. She's stunning. Every inch of her is perfection, and she's mine.

"Lie down." I pull her toward the bed. She scoots herself to the middle and props her head up on a pillow. I unbutton my shirt and toss it to the floor next to her panties, disposing of my undershirt and pants next. Her breasts are perky and nipples tight as I kneel on the bed next to her. Her breathing is ragged and her pupils dilated with want.

"So fucking beautiful." I run my hand down her chest between her breasts and to the flat expanse of her stomach. Soft white skin is speckled with goose bumps from my touch. I love how her body reacts to me. Her back arches slightly, and her knees fall apart. My cock throbs in anticipation when I see her bare and waiting for me.

Her hand reaches for my cock, but I brush it away. "Not yet," I mumble and position myself on the bed between her legs. I press her thighs open wide and run a finger through her glistening lips. She gasps at my touch, and I can't help but smile at how turned on and wet she is for me. I slip a finger inside her and then a second. She clenches gently and rocks her hips as my fingers fuck her. My thumb swirls small circles around her throbbing clit, and her back arches as I feel her climax building.

Pulling my fingers from her, I lean forward and press my mouth to her pussy. I lick and suck at her clit as I watch her body climb closer to the edge. She's fucking perfect. She palms her taut breasts, a pink flush crawling across her cheeks. Her eyes are closed, and her tongue dances across her bottom lip before she pulls it into her mouth as she moans.

Her legs begin to shudder as her release comes fast and quick, her moans turning to rapid gasps as she comes undone. I've never seen or tasted anything more exquisite in my entire life. I breathe and take a moment to collect myself, having almost blown my load just from watching her come.

Her arms lay limp on the bed, her legs still open for me. Her breathing begins to settle as I press the head of my cock against her wet opening.

Her eyes spring open and a smile tugs at her lips. "Need you," she mouths, and I slide into her.

Tight, warm, inviting, mine. All of her.

I make love to her with everything I have. I worship her body. I make love to her soul. In this moment, I make an unspoken commitment to her—I'll always love her and never let her go.

Sated, her eyelids finally fall closed. She lies in my arms, a tangle of limbs. I've never felt so close to anyone in my life. Her breathing slows. I press a light kiss to her forehead, then she rolls toward me and whispers, "Don't ever leave me again. I'm lost without you. I'm so tired of being lost, Alex."

"I won't. I promise," I tell her and press another kiss to the top of her head. I will do everything in my power to keep this promise.

She clings to me tightly while she falls asleep. As she falls deeper into slumber, her death grip loosens and I'm finally able to free myself. I'm restless and don't want to wake her, so I quietly leave the bed, pulling the covers over her.

Slipping into my office, I power up my computers and spend the next hour working. From messages back and forth with carriers and Navarro, I find out that deposits were made, guns were bought, and shipments of marijuana and heroin made it successfully across the border. I should be fucking ecstatic, but it eats at me.

I plug in the flash drive that I brought back from Mexico with me and sort through folders and files, reorganizing so they're more easily searchable by date. There's one folder titled "Research" that I've never seen before. Opening it, I find a series of subfolders all titled with a series of letters—JM, AME, and EA. My mouse hovers over JM, but before I can click on it, Emilia walks into the room with my bed sheet wrapped around her.

"What're you working on?" With small steps, she rounds the desk. I lean back in my chair, and she sits on my lap. There is nothing better than seeing Emilia in nothing but a sheet and sitting in my lap.

"Just work. I couldn't sleep." I sweep her long hair over her shoulder and trace her delicate collarbone with my fingertip. I feel her body tremble, and she tilts her head to the side. Smiling, I lean in and press a kiss to her neck, tracing small circles there with my tongue. I love her neck.

Suddenly, she lets go of the sheet and runs her fingers through my hair, stopping at the nape of my neck. Her tongue swipes my lower lip and I inhale sharply.

"Em," I say against her lips.

"Shh." She runs her nails down my chest. Reaching inside the waistband of my shorts, she grips my cock, running her thumb across the head. In one swift motion, I stand up and she wraps her legs around me. Work completely forgotten, I set her on the edge of the desk and pull off my shorts.

With one thrust, I'm deep inside her, and a yelp escapes her. It's hard and hungry. It's needy—I *need to be inside her.*

"Alex," she mumbles between heavy breaths. Her head falls back as I thrust harder into her. Her fingernails rip into my shoulders.

"I've never felt anything so good in my life, Emilia." She's wet and warm and soft, but it's more than sex, it's more than a mass of bodies—it's love I feel for her.

Her hips grind in motion to mine, and her breathing hitches. As she comes, she throws her body back onto the desk while I continue fucking her. Her face is flush and her nipples are tight.

"You feel so good," she whispers as I still inside her, not ready to finish.

"Wrap your legs around me."

She obeys, tightening her legs, her pussy clenching around me. I'm so close to losing it but manage to stave off my climax. I guide her body up and lift her. Her hand hits the keyboard as I pull her into my arms. I'm still buried deep inside her—my favorite place in the fucking world.

Then, over her shoulder, the computer monitor abruptly brightens, and my stomach drops when I see Emilia's face on the screen. There's a picture displayed on the screen that I've never seen before. I don't know why my father has a picture of her, but I know something is terribly wrong.

chapter fourteen

Sam

DON'T GET CLOSE. Don't let her in. Ignore my racing heart, my sweaty palms, and the throb in my cock. I repeat this mantra every hour, but I can't. Emilia has no fucking clue what she's in the middle of, or how she's going to be my ticket to take down the Estrada Cartel.

I slam the file folder closed and pinch the bridge of my nose.

Trey saunters up and leans against my desk. "How was dinner?"

"Good. Nice, actually." That's only a half truth. It was more than nice. It was perfect. *Don't let her in,* I tell myself once again. Fuck, I'm so screwed.

"Get any info?"

"None. I'm wondering if I'm chasing down the wrong lead. I don't think she knows what or who she's living with."

"She has a fucking tail. Andres Romo. She knows what's going on."

"I don't know, man." I rub my eyes. Part of me is dead set

on using her. The other part of me wants to rescue her.

"We need her," Trey says firmly.

I nod and lean back in my chair. Lacing my fingers behind my head, I kick my feet up onto my desk. "What if we can't get anything from her?"

"We will. Actually, *you* will." Trey smirks.

"She doesn't have a clue about her father, does she?" I ask Trey, who's picked up the file I have on Emilia and is flipping through the pages.

"Nah."

"So, why in the hell did Antonio Estrada pull her into his world? I don't understand."

"She's collateral, regardless. If he takes her out, maybe her daddy will feel guilty and throw out the case. It's a scare tactic, Sam. We've seen this a hundred times."

"Do you think he'll kill her?" My hands unconsciously clench around the edge of my desk.

"When has anyone walked away from the Estrada cartel alive?"

He's right. "Never."

"Exactly. Even the pussy Antonio Estrada hires for the night disappears for good when they leave. He cleans up his mess, though, and he does it well. We don't have shit on him other than the drug charges. We need more... guns, humans. We need it all to take them down. Which is why we need the girl before he does something to her."

"The girl has a name. Emilia," I grumble, agitated. Shaking my head, I say, "I don't know, though. Something doesn't feel right. Something about this just isn't adding up."

"What's not adding up is that we don't have anything." Now

he's agitated, running a hand through his hair. "We need intel from her, and fast. Antonio is up for a bail hearing in a couple days, and Martin isn't the judge setting bail. If he's got the cash, he'll be out."

"I'm working on it." I groan in frustration. "So, we've got Antonio Estrada in prison." I draw a chart on a piece of paper. Alex Estrada is his son who is running the organization. His girlfriend is Emilia Adams. Emilia Adams is Judge Martin's daughter. They're using her. But for what? She should be dead by now if they were sending a message to Martin."

"I don't know. Just do whatever it takes to get something. We've been coming up dry for months. Emilia's our girl." Trey pushes himself off my desk and walks away.

"She's not *our* girl, she's mine," I mumble to myself and open her file again.

"Cortez, status meeting in conference room A. Now!" Hale barks at me. He's the lead detective on this taskforce, and we meet daily to provide updates. Unfortunately, for weeks—make that months— I've had no updates.

If I don't get something soon, I'm fucked.

DETECTIVE HALE BRIEFS the joint taskforce with a few updates. Mostly nothing. I flip through my files, one on Antonio Estrada and one on Alex Estrada. One thing about the Estrada family is that they're spotless, except for Antonio's little slip-up. The kilo of cocaine he had in his truck when he tried to reenter the U.S from Mexico was enough to hold him for as long as we have. The

Estrada cartel does a fine job of flying under the radar. They're not flashy and they don't send public messages like many of the larger organizations. This has brought them much success. They're small but mighty. They move millions of dollars of drugs, guns, and people across the border every month. Antonio Estrada's net worth sits around fifty million and Alejandro Estrada is not far behind that.

Antonio runs the cartel, but Alejandro, also known as Alex, is the brains of the organization. He manages the "business," the money. He invests and does a fucking damn good job of keeping most of that money clean.

"Cortez?" A voice pulls me away from my thoughts.

"Yeah, sorry." I perk up.

"Any updates?" Hale asks, resting his hands on his hips.

"Not today. Getting closer. Hoping for something soon."

"Soon would be nice. Yesterday would've been fucking phenomenal." He scowls at me, and I can feel the tension in the room. They're looking for me to make the break, and I'd love nothing more than to put those fuckers behind bars for life.

"Look, if I push Emilia Adams too hard, she's going to pull away. Give me some time."

"Time is a luxury we don't have, Cortez."

I sigh and rub my eyes as Trey jumps in. "Shipment of guns was supposed to come through Nogales yesterday. It didn't happen. Intel in Mexico is telling us everything is on hold. I'm not sure what's happening, but there's been a change in their deliveries. They're onto us."

"Goddammit!" Detective Hale smacks the table. "I want those fucking guns. I want the driver. I want the truck. I want that entire goddamn organization taken out. Find out where the fucking guns are and when they're coming across the border." He stalks out of the conference room, slamming the door behind him. Trey and I pass a concerned look between us.

"Now seems like a great time to get some coffee," I tell Trey and push myself up from the table.

"Good luck," he mumbles.

"Thanks. I'm going to need it."

chapter fifteen

Emilia

"WHAT'S WRONG?" I feel Alex tense when I ask him this. Last night, after he brought me back to bed, he was distant, disconnected. He made love to me physically, but mentally, he was somewhere else.

"Nothing."

"Don't lie to me, Alex." I prop my head on my arm and trace his chest muscles.

He sighs loudly before pulling me closer. "I just have a lot on my mind."

"Like?"

"Em..." His voices pleads with me not to push him.

"I'm sorry. I'm just worried about you."

"I'm fine. I just have to get a few things taken care of this morning, and then I'll be home. You're calling in sick to work today. I need you here at the house. I have to take Andres with me." He leans in and presses a kiss to my lips. I love how he tells me what to do, then follows it up with a kiss.

I roll my eyes at him.

"I can't call in sick. They need me." Plus, I don't like being told what to do. Alex should know that by now.

"Em," he says, his voice tired.

"Fine," I concede begrudgingly. "Just today. I won't do this again, Alex." I give him a stern look, but his gleeful smile doesn't care.

"Good." He pushes my shoulder gently, urging me to my back. Rolling on top of me, he slides inside me and makes love to me. Sweet and caring. The Alex that went missing last night is back.

I TURN ON the shower in Alex's bathroom and step inside. There are showerheads that spray gentle streams of water from all directions, and the hot water massages my tired muscles. I inhale the steam, pulling the hot, moist air into my lungs.

Suddenly, I'm hit with a blast of cold air as Alex steps in with me. He stands under a showerhead across the way, his amber eyes fixed on me. I can see the defined lines of his abs as he lifts his arms to shampoo his hair. Tipping his head back into the stream, the suds roll down his firm, tanned body. His cock is semi-hard, lying against his thigh, and I want him inside me again. I'll never get enough of him.

He catches me looking and smiles before stepping forward. "Something you like?"

"Mmhmm," I mumble as he presses a sweet kiss to my lips.

"I want nothing more than to press you up against this

shower wall and fuck you senseless, Em, but I have a meeting I have to get to. Tonight, you won't be able to walk once I'm done with you." He squeezes my nipple gently, and I laugh.

With a good-natured expression, he takes a step back. "Take your time in here. Rosa is here and will have breakfast for you. I'll be back in a couple of hours."

I smile. "Okay."

"And remember, no leaving."

I roll my eyes. "Got it, warden."

He chuckles at that, then steps out of the shower, leaving me to wonder what the hell is going on that he's taking Andres with him. I don't let myself think for too long because then I'll worry.

I finish my shower and dress quickly. Rosa is in the kitchen, humming to Spanish music that's blaring from her phone. She shakes her hips as she pushes scrambled eggs around in a pan on the stove, and I giggle, watching her.

She startles when she sees me and shakes her wooden spoon at me. "Girl, don't go sneaking up on people."

"I didn't!" I raise my hands in surrender. "You're quite the dancer, Rosa," I joke with her.

Her laugh is loud and bellows through the open kitchen. "You're lucky I like you, Emilia." She shoves a plate full of scrambled eggs, bacon, and toast in front of me. "Coffee?"

"I would love some." She's so good to me. I envision if my mom was healthy, she would have been like Rosa. I smile at that thought.

"What time do you have to be to work?"

"I'm calling in sick today. My stomach is bothering me," I lie to her. I don't know if Alex told her I'd be here or not, and it's best to just lead on that I'm not feeling well.

"I can make you something else if that food is too heavy." She points to the plate.

I almost hug my plate. No way is she taking this delicious meal away from me. "This is fine, Rosa. Thank you." I smile at her.

"I have some errands to run and groceries to pick up. You feeling okay to be here alone?" she asks as she hand washes the dishes in the sink. I still don't understand why she doesn't use the dishwasher. I never had a dishwasher. If I could've avoided hand washing dishes, I would've.

"Yeah. I'll be fine. I'm just going to lie down and rest."

"Okay. Do you need me to pick up anything for your stomach? Pepto Bismol, ginger ale, or crackers?"

"I'm good, but thank you." She's too good to me.

My phone buzzes on the counter, and I see Sam's name on the screen. Swiping the home screen, I pull up his text. My stomach turns as I remember Alex's warning to stay away from him.

I had a really nice time last night.

Even with Alex's lingering warning and the revelation of who Sam really is, I can't help but smile. I actually had a really nice time too. It was nice talking to him and getting to know him. He's different from Alex in the sense that he's "safe" in a nine-to-five professional job kind of way. He's a mass-market man, whereas Alex is a niche market kind of man. I don't think Sam even knows I live with Alex, and I enjoyed the fact that I wasn't on edge or had to look over my shoulder like I sometimes do with Alex. But I love Alex. I don't love Sam. That much is clear to me.

Me too, I respond.

When can I see you again?

My heart races with that question. Because I don't know the answer, and I'm torn. I ignore him, but he responds quickly.

Is everything okay?

I sigh guiltily and text: *Just not feeling well. I'll message you later.*

There's a knock on the front door. Weird. Alex didn't say anything about anyone stopping by. I toss my phone aside and head to the front. When I see the peephole is covered with a hand, anxiety pools in my stomach. The deadbolt is locked, so I jog quickly to Alex's office to check the security cameras. Wiggling the mouse, the screen lights up, and I can see eight small frames from each of the eight different security cameras. Each frame rotates to a larger screen. Finally, I see that it's Saul outside. I shudder when I think of him and decide that I won't answer.

Sitting in the leather office chair, I hold my breath while I watch Saul on the screen. He presses his hand against the peephole and knocks with the other. When he gets no response, he opens his cell and walks away. I watch him take the stairs down to the parking garage before I lose him.

Blowing out a breath, I lean back in the chair, scanning the monitors several more times. And then… My breath hitches when an old picture of myself looks back at me. Alex has a picture of me? From my high school graduation?

"What the hell?" My lungs are in my throat.

It's the same picture I keep tucked inside the front of my journal, only in this picture, my mom has been cropped out. I close it out and find that it's inside a folder with other documents, files, and pictures. When I click on another image, a picture of my dad pops up. He's dressed in a tuxedo, obviously at an event. *My dad.* He's smiling—happy. Why does Alex have pictures of my family? My heart races as I click on another image. This time of my mom.

"Jesus Christ," I whisper, horrified.

With a shaky hand, I click on yet another image—a photo of my mom dead on the floor of our trailer, holding that gun. A gun I knew we never owned. Tears fill my eyes quickly and spill down my cheeks as I question everything I thought I believed about Alex. Why does he have these pictures? And why *this* picture? Oh my God, was he involved?

Nausea settles in, and my stomach begins twisting inside me. I run to the bathroom in my bedroom, barely making it before I spill the contents of my breakfast into the toilet. In between bouts of vomiting and crying, I manage to pull myself together. Fear and unease settle in the pit of my stomach as I hear the front door close and footsteps echoing down the hall. With a deep breath and one last swipe of powder to my nose, I know that I have to be strong and stay focused. I'm getting answers.

"Em?" I hear his voice and a chill runs up my spine.

I plaster a fake smile on my face and swallow down my fear. "In here," I answer him calmly. I stand in front of the large vanity, and I can see him in the mirror.

"What're you doing in here?" His brows are furrowed as he glances around my bathroom.

"Just freshening up," I lie.

He nods, deep in thought. "I'll have Rosa move your belongings over to my room. There's no sense in keeping your things here now that you're staying in my room." He says it so casually, and I freeze as I think about all of my items in his room and in his bathroom.

Finally, noticing my demeanor, he asks, "Is everything all

right? You look pale."

I turn to him and rest a hand on my stomach. "I'm glad I called in sick. My stomach has actually been bothering me."

He presses a palm to my forehead before pulling my head to him and resting his lips there instead. He presses a few small kisses to my forehead before releasing me. Bile rises from my stomach when his warm hands rest on my shoulders, but I swallow hard, forcing it down.

"You don't feel warm."

"Probably just a little stomach bug. I think I'm going to lie down." I wiggle out of his grasp and walk around him.

"I'll lie down with you, but I have something for you first." Alex pulls a small box out from his pocket and hands it to me. "Open it." He moves toward me, the scent of his cologne filling the air around us. It's soft and masculine and has the power to weaken my resolve, but it's the box sitting in my hand that has my knees shaking together.

My heart stammers in my chest as my fingers run across the smooth dark blue velvet case. With shaky hands, I lift the lid and there sits a beautiful gold necklace with a diamond encrusted compass charm dangling from the thin chain. I gasp. I've never owned a piece of jewelry in my life, let alone something this beautiful. I look up, and Alex has a sincere smile on his face as he watches me. I fake a smile again as I'm wondering if his smile is another lie.

I wonder what lie he'll tell next, and I wonder if it'll be the one to break me.

chapter sixteen
Alex

"ALEX," SHE WHISPERS quietly, running her fingers across the beautiful compass. "What is this for?" She bites her lip, and I can see her heart racing by the steady pulse of the vein in her neck.

Do I tell her the truth? The truth that I need her as much as she needs me? The truth that I don't want to live without her? The truth that she is the *only* good thing in my life?

The truth that I love her?

"Because you stayed," I finally say. "You loved me enough to stay. You don't know what that means to me." I reach out and brush a strand of hair off of her face, tucking it behind her ear. She flinches at my touch and pulls away slightly, but I see tears in her eyes—a sign of conflict.

My smile falters. "If you don't like it, I can return it."

"No," she says quickly, pulling the chain from the box. "I love it, but you didn't have to do this."

"I wanted to." *I'd do anything for you.*

She unhooks the clasp and reaches behind her neck. I turn

her around and remove the chain from her fingers, fastening the clasp and fixing her hair. The necklace sits perfectly on her chest.

"Em." I tip her chin up so she looks me in the eye. "It kills me to hear you say you have nobody. You'll always have me. You'll never be alone or lost again. I don't know if I believe in fate, but something brought us together at that hotel. I took one look at you and knew we needed each other."

Tears spill from her eyes, and she swats them away.

Before I lose my nerve, I tell her, "I love you, Emilia." Then she lunges into my arms and sobs into my chest. I've never been good at comfort, but if I could take away all of her pain, I would.

She clings to me as if she doesn't believe what I've said. "Alex," she stutters between breaths. "Before you say anything else, I need you to be honest with me." She slides her hand into mine and pulls me toward the couch in the living room. She sits but puts some distance between us. I notice her slouched shoulders and balled up fists in her lap.

"What's going on, Em?"

"Are you going to hurt me?" Her chin quivers.

"Never," I cut her off. "Why would you even ask me that?"

"The picture."

Shit. I swallow hard. "What picture, Emilia?" I play stupid. She saw the fucking picture.

"The picture of me on your computer. And the one of my dad, and my mom, dead. Why do you have those, Alex? What're you doing with them?" Her voice shakes.

Wait, what? I saw the one—of her. But that was it. "What're you talking about? Pictures of your mom and dad? I don't have pictures of your parents, Em. I don't even know who your parents are."

"You do. On your computer in your office. I saw them this afternoon."

"Shit." I rake my hands over my face. I knew something was wrong last night when I saw her picture, but the only man that has the answers I need is locked up, and I can't ask him.

"Tell me, Alex." Her voice is angry, her face sad. "If you love me, tell me the truth."

I fumble for words, helpless. "I don't know the truth, Emilia. That's the truth. I don't know." I know I need to get to that computer and see what else is on there, but I'm more worried about Emilia at the moment. "Here's what I can tell you. I transferred files from a computer in Mexico to a flash drive. That's where those photos came from. I haven't even had time to look at them."

"Whose computer did you transfer files from?" Her voice is clipped.

I scoot toward her on the couch, but she shifts back further. She looks fragile and frail, yet so strong. Beneath her tears is the most beautifully broken woman I've ever met. But instead of the truth, I'll break her with more lies.

"A business associate." I don't look at her as I spill lies. I can't tell her it was my father's computer. Before I can tell her the truth, I need to get answers for myself.

But she sees through my lie and jumps up from the couch, running into her room. I follow close behind, and she grabs her bag and begins shoving clothes into it.

"What're you doing?"

"Leaving," she snaps. My heart drops.

"No you're not, Emilia. I cannot lose you. I love you." I can't let her leave like this. *And I sure as fuck can't let her leave now.*

Not when I know my dad knows her whole fucking family. Something is not right here.

"Like hell, I'm not," she rages. "You said yourself if I tried to leave, you'd let me. I'm leaving. I can't trust you." Her voice shakes and her movements are clumsy. She's breaking down, losing control, but it's the words she just snarled at me that hurt me the most. *I don't trust you.* Those words cut me and my heart falls.

"Emilia. I'm the only person you can trust." I grab her arm and try to turn her to look at me. "Stop. You need to calm down and let me figure out what's going on."

"Don't touch me." She yanks her arm free and runs to the nightstand for her journal and an envelope. She pulls out cash and throws it on the bed. "That should cover everything I owe you." Then she hikes her bag onto her shoulder and stomps out.

"You don't owe me anything. Em, don't leave. I love you," I yell at her again. Anger and frustration—but mostly fear—course through me. If she walks out that door, I can't protect her. She's the first woman I've ever loved and I cannot lose her. "Emilia." I chase her out to the elevator. "Please."

She steps inside, clearly struggling to keep her emotions in check, but she's not stopping. She's not coming back to me. I can see it in her eyes—disgust.

"I love you, Em. Please. Stay. Let me figure this out. I'll get you answers," I beg her as the elevator doors close in my face.

I PACE THE condo, my stomach in knots. She left her phone on the bed next to the cash, so I have no way of reaching her. I'm panicking. Fucking panicking. I've never felt like this before. I step over the broken vases and the picture I tore off the wall in my rage a moment ago, and I stomp into my office to finally look at those files.

I click on the folder titled "Research" and the image titled "EA." It's Emilia. The initials of her first and last name identify the image, Emilia Adams. JM stands for Jeffrey Martin, the judge overseeing my father's case. I recognize his photo immediately. As I click through more photos, I find more of Judge Martin and more of Emilia. Emilia mentioned seeing her mother *and* her father. My stomach flips when I make the connection. Jeffrey Martin. Judge Jeffrey Martin is Emilia's father.

"Holy shit," I mumble and rub my chin. Emilia is a pawn in this game, and she's played right into my father's hand. I continue clicking through a few more pictures, but it's the last photo that sends chills down my spine and bile rising into my throat. It's of Emilia's mother lying dead in a pool of her own blood on the trailer floor.

"The fuck." I shut my eyes and close the image. Picking up my cell, I scroll through my contacts, finding the name of the only person I shouldn't trust, but I do. I press send on the screen and listen to the phone ring.

"I need to talk to you," I say, sputtering out a location to meet before hanging up. Then I toss my phone on the desk and bury my face in my hands, fighting back the tears that have been on the brink of breaking free all day.

chapter seventeen

Emilia

I STAND OUTSIDE the church that called to me like a beacon in the darkness. I didn't know where else to go, and I knew this was where I needed to be. Adjusting my bag on my shoulder, I tip my head back and look up at the bell that strikes loudly at the top of the hour.

"Emilia?" I hear his voice before I see him.

Father Mark slips out of a side door and locks it behind him. "Is everything all right?"

I shake my head, words failing me again. He must think I'm an idiot.

Eyeing my bag, his eyes become sympathetic, and he invites me inside. I follow him in and sit in the last pew, setting my bag on the ground next to me. We sit in silence for minutes before Father Mark turns to me.

"Where are you going to go?"

So, he knows I'm leaving. I feel a lump in my throat and shrug. I shrug because I don't have an answer. He nods quickly and drops his eyes to his hands, which are laced together in his lap. "Alex is a complicated man, Emilia. When he told me about you, I prayed you wouldn't get caught up in everything." He pulls a hand free and whirls it around the air between us.

"You know about his business?" I blink at the floor. I can't believe Father Mark would know.

"All too well." He sighs. "Emma, Alex's mother, used to confide in me about how the business was destroying her family. She was so worried about what her boys were being exposed to—drugs, guns, violence. She grew up in a nice family not too far from here. They were a poor family, but a nice and loving family. Emma wanted that for her children; a loving, nurturing environment. And Antonio gave her everything she didn't have growing up—money, a nice house, a car—but she quickly realized what the cost of those luxuries was. Her family. She wanted to take the boys and leave it all behind, but Antonio wouldn't hear of it. He loved her, but he loved the business more."

He shakes his head sadly, then continues, "She came to me for help. Asked me to get the boys out of school so she could take them and leave. It wasn't unusual for me to pull children from class and have them help me here in the parish. I had a funeral I had to be at, so I told her I'd help her the following day. She was killed that afternoon. I never got to help her." His body sags with age-old secrets and a grief I know all too well.

He keeps his eyes downcast and his voice low. "I know it wasn't my fault, but to this day, I carry the guilt of knowing her death could've been prevented if she'd left that day, had I helped her get those boys out of the parish school. It would've taken me five minutes…" He sighs. "Instead, I watched a family be destroyed, one son handed over to his aunt and uncle, and another left behind to be raised in a life of horror."

Horror… Alex never chose this life. I know that. Still…

"Emilia, I don't know where you're going, but go. Get away from here."

"I am." I just need to figure out where.

"The further away the better." He places his hand on mine, giving it a fatherly pat. "Take all the time you need here, Emilia. And if there's anything I can do to help, please ask."

"Thank you, Father."

He offers a kind smile and leaves. I lose track of time as I sit in the wooden pew. The church grows darker as night settles in, the only light coming from the overhead lights that shine down on the altar in the distance.

I pray again to a God that probably won't hear me—but I beg him for direction, for clarity. I even kneel and rest my forearms on the back of the pew in front of me, bowing my head in silence as if the answers to my prayers will suddenly come.

I hear the door behind me open, but I'm too lost in my thoughts and my own sadness to care. Moments later, a hand rests on my shoulder, and I raise my head.

Sam? How did he know I was here?

"Hey," he says quietly. "Need a friend?" He spots my bag on the ground and looks back to me.

"I do."

"Come on." He reaches for my hand. "Let's go." With his other hand, he grabs my bag and we walk out the back of the church and into the hot Phoenix night. Another summer monsoon is brewing and lightning reaches across the dark sky to the south. Sam guides me to his car, which is parked on the street. As I settle in, I glance back and see Father Mark at the top of the stairs, watching us before he retreats inside.

"Did Father Mark tell you where to find me?" I ask, curious.

He shakes his head slowly, but keeps his eyes focused straight ahead. "No."

"Then how'd you know I was here?"

"Alex told me."

SAM AND I sit at a small table in the kitchen of his house in an old historical neighborhood of downtown Phoenix. The bungalow-style house has been remodeled, but touches of the old have been left behind to complement the new modern interior. Sam and I haven't spoken since he told me it was Alex that told him where to find me.

In my mind, I try to weave together the web of lies that have been spun to me by both of them, but I'm coming up empty.

Sam sits silently, waiting for me to ask questions, while I sit equally as silent and wait for him to offer me answers. Neither of us is willing to go first. We're both headstrong and not willing to budge. Maybe these are our greatest strengths, or maybe our biggest downfall.

It's a showdown. Who will break first? Of course it'll be me, but until I do, Sam and I shift uncomfortably in our chairs. Sam sends emails or texts from his phone. The muscles in his forearms stretch as he rolls his fingers on the table and then his foot begins a light tapping on the floor. When he tires of that, he runs his hands through his hair and rubs his temples, a light groan emanating from the back of his throat. I take note of everything he does. He's a beautiful man. Complex and dedicated, waiting out my stubbornness. I find these qualities attractive and frustrating all in the same breath.

"Why would Alex call you?" There they are, the first words I've spoken in hours, and I submitted first. I'll let him win the battle of willpower because I need answers.

His eyes dart from the wall he was studying to me. "He needed me."

"That's a lie. He doesn't need you," I snarl. "He doesn't trust you."

He exhales loudly and rubs his chin. "You're right. He doesn't."

"Then why would he call you?" I demand.

"I don't know, Emilia. I'm trying to figure all of this out myself. But when he said *you* needed me, I knew I had to find you."

"Why?" I frown, growing more agitated by the second.

"Because I care about you." His face is conflicted, as if it pains him to say that.

"You don't even know me," I whisper.

"I probably know you better than you know yourself." His eyes dance between mine. He runs his hand over his face and sighs deeply.

"Does he know I'm with you?" I ask, my voice strained.

"No. Do you want me to tell him?"

"No." *It would hurt him.* Damn him. Even with all of his lies, I still don't want to hurt him.

"I'm sure he already knows anyway." He shakes his head, annoyed. "For years, we've watched each other's every move. He knows you're here."

It wouldn't surprise me. Alex has always seemed to know my every move. Of course that's because he's always had his goons following me.

Sam smirks suddenly, like he can see the wheels turning inside my head, see how frustrated and torn I am about everything. Maybe even how torn I am between him and Alex. It's stupid. I love Alex. I don't love Sam—but there's an attraction to Sam.

The room has gone silent again, and I bury my face in my hands. "So tell me. You coming into the café to see me, and our dinner together... that was all professional, wasn't it?"

He stares long and hard at me before his face softens. "It started as professional, Emilia... but then it became personal. I told you I care about you." I don't want to believe him, but I do.

I grit my teeth. "I didn't know anything about Alex or the business until a few days ago, Sam."

"I know," he admits. "It took me all of three minutes to know you didn't have a clue."

I scowl at him. "I won't give you anything on Alex or the business. So, if that's why I'm here, I'd like to leave."

"You're not going anywhere, Emilia," he says firmly, his eyes warning me.

SAM GRABS A blanket and pillow from a closet in the hallway and tosses it on the couch. "I'll sleep out here and you can take my bed."

I huff, although there's no point in arguing. He's the epitome of a true gentleman; he'd never let me sleep on the couch. To be honest, I don't have the fight in me tonight to argue anyway.

I saunter into the bedroom and collapse into Sam's bed. My tense muscles finally begin to unwind, and I inhale deep breaths in hopes of calming my mind. Rolling to my side, I watch the lightning stretch across the sky through the window. I watch the lightning and the clouds roll in before the wind finally takes hold, branches whipping through the air and the roof creaking as the intensity picks up.

Thunder cracks loudly and reminds me of the summer storms we'd get in Illinois. Mom and I would lie together on her bed and listen to the rain and wind and pray that our trailer would make it through each storm.

As the storm outside strengthens, I slide out of the bed and stand near the window. The air outside is thick with dust, and the first drops of rain slap against the window. Suddenly, a dark figure moving across the yard catches my attention, and I scream, jerking out of view.

"Emilia!" Sam comes barreling through the bedroom door, holding a gun and wearing only a pair of boxer briefs and his unbuttoned dress shirt. "What happened?"

I'm pressed against the wall, my fingers digging into my thighs. "There's someone outside."

"Get down," he orders me. I crouch down and Sam moves quickly to the side of the window. He glances discreetly outside, his eyes scanning the yard. "Stay here and don't get up until I come back."

Fear sets in and my entire body begins to shake uncontrollably. This is the first time I've felt real danger, and the combination of adrenaline and fear sends me into a state of panic.

I huddle in the corner of the room, my arms wrapped tightly around my legs, and I rock slightly back and forth to remain calm.

A few minutes later, Sam finds me and kneels next to me on the floor. "It's fine, Emilia. You're fine." He wraps a gentle hand around my bicep. "I checked the security feed, and there was no one out there."

I frantically shake my head. "There was. I saw someone, Sam. I'm not lying."

"I know you're not," he consoles me. "But I think maybe it was a shadow from a tree, or you're just exhausted and seeing things."

"I'm not seeing things," I snarl at him.

"Hey, it's okay." He pulls me into him. My head rests against his bare chest, and I can smell the light musky scent of his skin. It's clean but masculine. His embrace is comforting, and I sink into him, enjoying the temporary comfort of his arms.

"I'm going back to the living room. If you need me, call for me."

"Stay with me." I need him. I love Alex, but right now, I need Sam.

His eyes are conflicted and his posture hesitant, but he nods and sets his gun on the nightstand. Crawling into the bed, he lies down on his back, as close to the edge as possible, arms above his head. His dress shirt falls open and I can see the tight curves of his muscles and a light sprinkling of dark hair just below his navel.

I slide back to the other side of the bed and lie on my side, facing him, my knees pulled up to my chest. We lie together in silence, our eyes locked. That eye contact and our breathing are the only ways we communicate with each other, but we can read each other without muttering a single word.

For the first time since meeting Sam, I see his face etched with an unknown pain. It's there, written across his face like a map, and I want to ask questions, but I don't. Silence fills the space between us, until the physical distance is too great. Hesitantly, I reach out and rest my hand on his chest, just over his heart. He holds his breath as my fingers come into contact with his soft, warm skin, then he lowers an arm and wraps my hand in his, giving it a gentle squeeze and pulling me closer. He holds my hand until we both fall asleep.

THE FAINT SOUND of a phone ringing pulls me from a deep sleep. Sam is on his stomach. Long, relaxed breaths tell me he's still asleep. I gently slide my arm out from under his and try my best to get out of the bed without waking him.

"It's too early for you to be awake," he grumbles.

I startle. "I was trying not to wake you."

He rolls to his side and half opens one eye, while I sit on the edge of the bed. "Come here." He tugs me back, his arm finding my waist, and we both lie on our sides, facing each other. "Stay with me." His voice is raspy and his hair is messy, but there's nothing unsexy about this man in the morning.

"I can't, Sam. I'm sure it's a conflict of interest with your case… but I made up my mind last night. I'm going to Oregon."

And there's that pain again. "What's in Oregon?"

"The ocean," I whisper to him. I remember telling Alex about Oregon and what his response was. *"If you ever get the chance to go to Oregon, go."*

Sam runs his fingers along my jawline, over my lips, and up my cheeks. "I'd really like you to stay... with me," he says as I shift on the bed. He pulls me even closer, and I can feel his warm breath sweep across my cheek as he exhales. As he presses a kiss to my forehead, I close my eyes.

"I want to kiss you here." He presses another kiss to my forehead. "And here." His lips brush against my cheekbone. "And here." He pulls my bottom lip into his, and I gasp. "And I want to touch you, Emilia." His hand gently rubs my arm. My body betrays me and reacts to his touch, but as I close my eyes, I envision Alex's hands on my body and Alex's lips on mine.

"I can't," I whisper against his lips.

"You can, Em," he insists.

The phone in the other room begins ringing again, and Sam sighs loudly, grudgingly pulling away and sitting up.

"You should probably get that," I say quietly just as it stops ringing.

"I'll call them back. Do you want coffee?" He stands and stretches, then steps out.

"That'd be great. I'm going to shower really quick, but I'll be out in a minute."

I stumble into the attached bathroom and close the door behind me. While the shower runs, I quickly brush my teeth and then step into the stream of water. It's hot and scalds my skin and temporarily washes away the guilt I feel for letting Sam kiss me. Without changing the temperature, I lather up a washcloth and wash my face and body before quickly washing and conditioning my hair.

A moment later, there's a light rap on the door just as Sam's voice comes through. "I have to run out for a bit, Em. I'm setting a mug of coffee here for you."

I stick my head out from behind the curtain just as Sam reaches in and sets the steaming mug on the counter. "Thanks!" I respond and shut off the water, wrapping my hair in a thick towel and patting my body dry with another. As I wait for the mirror to de-fog, I sip on the hot coffee. It's perfect, and within minutes, begins to energize me. In the bedroom, I pull on a pair of panties and throw on a sundress.

With an arm full of wet towels, I walk back toward the bathroom, but a tall chest of drawers catches my attention. It's not actually the chest, but the picture that sits on top of it. With a shaky hand, I pick up the photo and gasp. But… *It can't be.* In a matter of seconds, my worlds collide and everything I thought I knew about Alex and Sam comes to a screeching halt.

chapter eighteen
Alex

I PACE THE kitchen, waiting for Sam to arrive. I fucking hate waiting. I'm impatient and I'm used to everything magically appearing within minutes—until yesterday. Sam, however, is on his own timeline. Fucking bastard. When Emilia left, she turned my world upside down. I had a plan; I just needed a little more time to execute it.

I eye the stack of folders on the kitchen island and the flash drive with every last detail about the Estrada family business. Lacing my fingers behind my head, I look up at the ceiling. My stomach clenches, and I inhale a deep, cleansing breath as I try to settle my nerves.

Finally, there's a firm knock at the door. "'Bout time," I mumble as I hurry to the front. And as the door swings open, I see that Sam is standing there, his hand gripping his holstered gun.

"You won't need that," I grit out as I step back and hold the door open for him.

Sam looks over his shoulder before stepping over the threshold and into my condo. He lets out a whistle as he heads down the hall and into the main living area. "Murder, guns, and drugs do a man good, huh? Nice to see you living so well." His voice drips with sarcasm.

"Fuck off, Sam."

He chuckles, although I can tell he's mentally taking note of everything in my condo. "So, I'm not usually one for making house calls with criminals, but since we both have an *interest* in Emilia, I'm assuming that's why you called me here?"

Just the sound of her name rolling off his tongue makes me violent. I clench my jaw and take a deep breath as I try to keep my composure. Rubbing the back of my neck, I close my eyes and give my decision one final thought. It's now or never. I'm in or out. Both have dire consequences.

"I'm ready," I say, my voice steel.

"For what?" he sneers.

"To make a deal."

His eyes widen in shock, and he props both hands on his hips, holding back his suit jacket. "Why now?"

"For Emilia." Anything for her. *Because she's everything.*

He's silent for a moment. "You're making a deal because of Emilia?"

"For Emilia," I repeat. Not because of, but for her. I nod and swallow against my dry throat.

"Well, I'll be damned," he mutters and shakes his head slowly. "So what do you want?"

I take a deep breath. "I'll give you everything for immunity from prosecution and witness security for Emilia and me. I keep my cash assets. You can seize the properties. I'll give you everything. Most of it's in these folders and on that flash drive." I gesture to the stack of file folders on the kitchen island, the flash drive on top.

He smirks and rubs his chin. "I'll have to take this back and see. You know I don't have the authority to approve a deal."

"I know." I clench and unclench my hands, so fucking nervous I don't know what to do with myself. Sam holds the key to my future, and I don't like trusting anyone with my future. "But it needs to happen fast. I need to get Emilia out of here."

"A deal like this doesn't happen overnight, Alex. You're a smart man. You know this. This could take months at the very minimum."

Goddammit. "We don't have months."

His face turns hard. "Well, you should've thought about that before you involved Emilia in your business."

Fuck you. Although he's right, I hate that he's right. "She was involved before I came along, and she didn't even know it. If I hadn't found her, she'd be in the desert somewhere with a fucking bullet in her head." I shut my eyes tightly at that reality, then open them back up, staring him down. "I had no idea until yesterday that Judge Martin was her father."

Sam's eyes narrow on me. "I find it very hard to believe that it was only two days ago that you found out Jeffrey Martin was her father."

I throw my hands out. "I honestly had no idea. I don't even think *she* knows her father is Judge Martin." I roll my neck, trying to relieve some of the tension in my neck and shoulders. "I was in Mexico last week and pulled files from the computer at the house.

When I got back, I found Emilia's picture in a folder with Judge Martin's. There were also pictures of her mother." I have Sam's attention now. He's listening to every word. For once, I think he believes me.

"Here." I stride over and pull the top file folder off the stack, sliding it across the granite counter to him.

He opens the file and looks up at me before flipping through the stack of pictures.

"The last one." I pause and take a deep breath.

"Jesus fucking Christ," Sam growls as he picks up the picture. It's the one of Emilia's mother, a bullet hole in her head. And that's not even the part that's disturbing. He sees exactly what I see. He knows what I now know.

That picture is almost an identical copy of my mother's crime scene photo from twenty years ago—the way the body is positioned, the gun in her hand—all of it is identical.

"He did it. He did all of it," Sam says, his voice eerily quiet and horrified.

I nod my head slowly in agreement with Sam. "I was in denial about Mom's murder." It's the first time Sam and I have talked about her since the day my aunt and uncle took him away from us, from me and our father. My dad did a great job teaching me to hate Sam. He made it clear that Sam didn't have it in him to run our business. He wasn't smart enough or strong enough. Problem is, my dad knew better. My dad knew that Sam was smarter than all of us.

Sam slides into a chair at the kitchen counter and drops his head into his hands. We sit for a moment before I speak up. "I never wanted to believe he would do that to her... to us," I say, my voice pained. "I just kept telling myself he was innocent."

Now, I'm not sure how I never saw my father's lies, what was right in front of me this whole time.

"He's a fucking pig," Sam says, disgusted.

"I started piecing everything together. Dad killed Em's mom as a message to Judge Martin. Only Emilia told me they've had no contact with him since the day he found out Emilia's mom was pregnant."

Sam raises his head. "So, Dad killed her for nothing. Judge Martin doesn't give a fuck about his ex-girlfriend from twenty-some years ago. The only thing that accomplished was leaving Emilia with no one."

I nod, and he blows out a breath.

"I need to take this information and see if we can get it to the judge before his bail hearing," Sam jumps up quickly.

"Too late," I say, feeling furious and helpless. "His hearing was this morning. I haven't heard from the attorney, but if it went well, he's processing out right now."

"Fuck." Sam slaps the counter with his open hand. "I need time!"

"Everything is in those files. They're yours as long as you can give me what I want. I'll talk. I'll give you written and verbal statements and any physical evidence you need." I run a hand over my face.

Sam pinches the bridge of his nose. "Let me get to the office and see what I can do. This would've been helpful a couple weeks ago." He scowls at me.

"A couple weeks ago, I didn't know what I know now," I shout, feeling riled up.

There's a loud knock on the door, and Sam jumps, positioning himself with his hand on his gun. "Expecting someone?" he asks, stepping into the kitchen and out of view from the front door.

"No," I say as I approach the door. Through the peephole, I see Emilia as she pounds on the door again. Flinging the door open, I immediately see anger and hurt in her eyes. "Em..."

"How many more are there?" she spits at me.

"How many what?" I'm sure whatever it is, it's true. And whatever reaction I get from her, I deserve.

"Lies. How many more?" Her eyes are full of unshed tears. I want to reach out and touch her, to pull her into my arms, but she's angry. "Were you honest with me about *anything?*"

"Come inside," I urge her, and she steps inside the door. I slam it behind her.

"There are two men on this earth that I was learning how to trust, Alex. You and Sam."

I look over her shoulder and see Sam stepping forward from the kitchen. I fucking hate that she trusts Sam and I can feel the bile rise from my stomach. He stands quietly behind her as she speaks. She doesn't know he's here.

"And both of you have done nothing but lie to me." Her voice breaks.

"Em," Sam says quietly, pulling her attention to him. She turns around quickly and faces him. "Of course you're here!" She raises an arm in exasperation.

"What is this about?" Sam steps forward toward her.

"The picture."

"What the hell is going on? Please explain this to me, because I'm confused as hell," I say as her eyes dart back and forth between Sam and me.

"I think it's safe to say we're all confused right now." Sam sighs. "Let's sit down and talk. Alex and I can fill you in on a few things."

"I'm not sure that's such a good idea." The voice behind us is low and demanding.

Sam freezes, Emilia frowns, and I turn to fucking ice all in one second.

Slowly, we all turn to find Saul and my father standing just inside my door.

"Emilia, come here. Now!" Sam pulls his gun from the holster on his hip, while I step in front of my father, distracting him so that Emilia can safely get to Sam. Saul has a pistol aimed at Sam, but he watches me closely.

"What is this, a goddamn family reunion?" My dad laughs, but I see the anger coursing through him. The vein in his neck throbs as he glances between Sam and me.

"Antonio," Sam says coolly, refusing to call our father anything personal. "Who'd you bribe to get bail? Or maybe I should be asking if Judge Anderson is on your payroll now? There's no way in hell you should've been offered bail."

I shoot Sam an annoyed look. Now is not the time to piss off our father or agitate him further.

"Agent Cortez." My dad smirks when he says "Cortez." It's my mother's maiden name and the last name of my aunt and uncle who raised Sam after my mother was murdered. "Nice to see you outside the confines of a jail interview room. Here for business or pleasure?" He cocks his head and looks at Emilia, the smirk falling from his face. "It appears that this may be the first time you two actually have a common interest."

My dad steps around me and, to my horror, approaches Sam and Emilia. When I try to follow, Saul steps in to block me.

"Look at what we have here." My father's gravelly voice echoes around us as he approaches Emilia. Sam steps in front of her, and my dad lets out a huff. "I just wanted a closer look."

"There's nothing to see," Sam grits out, Emilia clinging to the back of his jacket. She's afraid, and instead of me, she's holding on to Sam. I push Saul out of the way and lunge toward my father.

"Stay away from her," I snarl at him through gritted teeth. Suddenly, I hear the click of a gun safety and feel the hard metal barrel resting against the back of my head.

"Everyone, stop." Emilia's voice is weak and timid, but she steps out from around Sam.

What the fuck are you doing? No!

My father chuckles, low and evil. "I can see why my son and Agent Cortez are both attracted to you," he says as he pulls a piece of her hair into his fingers. She jerks away, but my father only chuckles again. "Feisty. Just like your mother."

"Don't…" I warn my father, but Saul presses the gun harder into the back of my skull.

"What about my mother?" she asks, her voice breaking, her eyes horrified.

He comes up close to her face. "I said you're feisty like her. She put up a good fight until she finally realized it was just easier to submit. Sorry to leave that mess for you, but sometimes sending an important message gets messy."

A guttural cry comes from the back of Emilia's throat. "You did it?" she screams at my father and falls to her knees. "Why? She was all I had." She struggles to catch her breath in between sobs. Everything in me longs to run to her.

"Em," I try to comfort her with my voice, but her arms are wrapped around her waist and she continues to gasp for air.

"You son of a bitch," she stutters between ragged breaths.

Sam's gun remains pointed at my father, and I see the fight in his eyes—keep the gun on my father or comfort Emilia. Smartly, he chooses the safest option for all of us—keeping my father contained at gunpoint.

"Sam, I need you to take Emilia and leave." I look to my father and expect him to listen to me, to let Sam and Emilia leave.

But he smirks. "Son, no one is going anywhere. I'm in charge again. My business. My call."

I watch Sam, and I can tell he's waiting for the opportune time to make a move. My father's eyes flicker to the large stack of file folders on the island, and he glances at me. His look reveals two things—that he's afraid I was about to give Sam everything… and that I was about to betray him. Everything about our business is in those folders and on that flash drive. Business associates, traffic routes, federal officials who've accepted money under the table to let us run our business. This information will crush careers outside of the cartel and destroy relationships my father has spent decades building.

Part of me panics as I watch him walk to the stack of folders, and part of me is glad he'll find out that I don't give a shit about this business. He pulls a file folder off the top of the pile and opens it, scans the page, then closes it. He pulls another folder down and repeats the same steps. He does this two or three more times, and my eyes bounce between him, Sam, and Emilia.

"Of my two sons, I chose you, Alejandro. You were the

obedient one. You were the one with the potential to grow this business. You were the one with brains," he snarls his insult at me. "But you're willing to give it all up, aren't you? This!" He smacks his hand on top of the folders. "This is how you repay me for everything I've provided you? Everything I've given you? You're going to betray and hand this over to your brother after everything I've done for you?" He waves his hands around the room, as if showcasing my condo.

"Why?" he asks, his eyes now reeking of betrayal. "Why would you give up our business?"

Saul nudges the base of my skull, a firm reminder that he's there and a prompt to answer my father.

"Answer me, son!"

"Emilia." It's as simple as that. I'd give it all up for her, for the chance to live a normal life with her.

Still on the floor, she raises her head and her eyes dart between me, my father, the stack of files, and back at me. A look of understanding begins to resonate, and she finally gets it. I'm doing this for her—for us.

My father is shaking with anger as he begins cursing in Spanish. He circles the island and rushes toward me. I brace myself for what's to come.

He takes a deep breath before he speaks. "Saul, give me the gun."

I feel the press of the gun pull away from my head, and I watch, horrorstruck as he leans around me and hands it to my father. My father releases the magazine, checking to see how many bullets are there. Then, snapping the magazine back in place, he raises the gun and points it at my chest. Of course he wouldn't shoot me in the head. That would be too easy. Painless. He wants to make me suffer.

I look my father in the eyes. I know this is how he handles business. I've always been business to him. Never a son, never something he loved. He loves nobody—just his business.

"Don't do it, Antonio," Sam warns, an edge of panic to his steely voice.

Suddenly, out of the corner of my eye, I see Emilia stand up behind Sam. "Please," she pleads with my father. "Don't."

They say things happen so quickly that, when faced with life-threatening situations, you don't have time to react. I now know that's true.

I hear the front door open and see flashes of light all at the same time. My ears ring as gunfire erupts, and I feel an immense pressure on my chest. Em is screaming and falls to the floor next to me. She's crying and reaching for me as Sam yells at her and pulls her away. I want to hold her. I promised her she'd never be alone again, but I lied. Again. It's what I do. It's what I've always done.

I see her hands reaching out for me and her long hair falling in waves around her stricken face. *So beautiful.* She doesn't even know how beautiful she is.

When I realize what's happening, I accept my fate. Like so many men before me, it's my turn to die.

I lay my head back on the floor. My dad is standing over me, and for the first time, I find conflict in his eyes—disappointment mixed with anger and sadness. He points the gun at my head, and I close my eyes. I hear Andres yell, and more gunfire rings out. It's then that warmth overtakes me and blood soaks through my shirt.

People say death is scary, and I used to be scared. I used to fear death. But death doesn't scare me anymore.

I welcome it.

TO BE CONTINUED
in
bound by lies...

acknowledgements

My family: Your love and support means everything. Thank you for dealing with my crazy, and loving me through it.

Amy: I don't know what I'd do without you. Thank you for *everything* my friend.

Megan: You made this a better story. Thank you for forcing me to dig deeper and write more.

To my fabulous readers: Your encouragement is what drives me. Thank you for the kind words and messages. Keep them coming!

connect with rebecca shea

www.rebeccasheaauthor.com

Sign up for Rebecca Shea's newsletter
for updates on new releases.
http://eepurl.com/Y3X81

Follow Rebecca Shea on Facebook:
www.facebook.com/rebeccasheaauthor

Follow Rebecca Shea on Twitter:
@beccasheaauthor

Email: rebeccasheaauthor@gmail.com

also by rebecca shea

Unbreakable Series

Unbreakable

Undone

Unforgiven

48064167R00156

Made in the USA
San Bernardino, CA
15 April 2017